# The One-Legged Barber

## and selected short stories

# The One-Legged Barber

## and selected short stories

by

**perry neel**

for James Mersmann,

who opened my eyes to the world...

"Wherever and however we live,
each of our hearts is a hand grenade
and all the pins are pulled.
        *After Visiting Pompeii*
        James Mersmann


"The realization that life is absurd and
cannot be an end, but only a beginning."
        Albert Camus


"It does not matter if
I am going anywhere;
I'm going there quick
and I'm leaving a track."
        *Mel Divides the Waters*
        James Mersmann

# *Acknowledgments*

Each character from these stories, in his or her own way, struggles for a moment of lucidity. In circumstances, sometimes self-created, sometimes not, they are looking for an epiphany. Part of the dilemma is that the world will move on in its inexorable way. That is a given. And they know that. As do we. But the greater portion is the moment where an insight is achieved, one that burns like a match struck in a room of darkness. Only briefly, though brightly, you can understand the predicament. And that is all you have to hold onto, and you grip the match, tight, till your fingertips burn.

I have been sitting on these stories, for reasons I cannot fathom, for the greater part of a quarter of a century. For similarly obscure reasons, I have decided to set them free. Maybe as the years wind down, one longs to leave some sort of legacy. But the fact that these old pages started turning up in bookshelves, in file folders, even in the laundry room, maybe signaled their yearning to be let go. So, like finding a bird in the house, I have opened the window and I'm shooing them out...

There is not much here. Maybe I am a minimalist? Though frequently coins, dust, gravel, an absent god, or a miscreant grandmother shows up.

Thanks to all who care.  And all who have cared about me including Tom, Jim, Tina, Anne, and Sandy, all of whom encouraged my work.  Tex for all the editing. Thank you to Marlena for helping with formatting. Thank you to Aine for her assistance with formatting and for the book cover layout.  And John Bell who created a masterful original painting for my cover art.  I only hope the stories live up to the cover.

To Rachael and Shelly, though you have absolutely nothing to do with any of this.  Well, Shelly did suggest I do it.  And helped immensely with such nuisances as bringing this project to publication.  But thanks.  Just for being here.

Perry Neel
Staunton, Virginia
2014
oneleggedbarber.weebly.com

# Contents

# The One-Legged Barber

## and selected short stories

## The One-Legged Barber

The dust coating was a regular feature of the working class neighborhood appropriately named Powderly. Although we lived in the West End of Birmingham, also blue-collar territory, the residents of Powderly worked the lower end of the labor force. In West End, our fathers being railroad engineers and butchers, we could rightfully look down on the oil and soot covered workers who clocked out to return to their little dust coated shotgun houses in Powderly.

But such social distinctions were as hazy as the skies over Powderly to a young boy of six. I knew that the Alpha-Portland Cement plant belched a continuous cloud for years over the small neighborhood. It took until college for the fantastic sight of this urban dust storm to give way to the concern over what it must have done to these poor folks to breathe the stuff for a lifetime.

In ways, Birmingham was as socially intricate as India. Even as a child I knew that working class families found some comfort in knowing there were lower castes than their own. Union labor bosses over the mountain and factory owners in Pittsburgh and Atlanta did their best to keep their advantage of cheap workers. Still, we had it better than some. New cars, color TVs, and home additions pacified most of the West End families. It's what we worked for. And if we didn't have much we still had more than the folks in Powderly.

That's how most families saw it. But not my father. Old black and white TV, clunker used cars, and paneling in the den - that was my father. Our West End standards were too lofty for him. And what made me so familiar with that dusty neighborhood was not the lower rung it occupied from West End. We didn't go there to boast our superiority. It was our monthly haircut, 75 cents there, compared to $1 in West End. Arant's Barber Shop with its rainbow colored array of hair tonic bottles in the window rack and penny gumball machine by the door was our regular destination for a trim. So we drove the old green Studebaker once a month through this suburban dust bowl to have Mr. Arant wrap the stiff barber bib and pin it around our necks, my brother and me, and sit in silence while my father and the barber talked. I don't really remember the conversations, probably baseball, George Wallace, and the weather. Just Mr. Arant's deep, throaty voice and the smells - hair tonic and talcum powder. Dutifully, my brother Tommy and I took our turns, sitting on the board laid across the arms of the barber chair. My father went third. While we in that order waited, Tommy and I quietly scratched our necks from the prickly little hairs that managed to sneak under the bib. Then, we always stood in unison as my father got out of the chair to pay Mr. Arant. We knew he would turn, and without our asking, offer us a penny each for the gumball machine. Our reward for good behavior. Before shoving our pennies in the slot and pushing the lever to release a shower of bright colored gumballs down the chute, we checked to see if they were the new "Lincoln Memorial" pennies or the old "One Cent" kind. Sometimes there would be more than a just allotment of white gumballs. I liked the purple ones, supposedly grape. My brother and I found the bitter peppermint white ones offensive, but having inherited our father's frugality, we chewed them, too.

On this one occasion as the Studebaker turned into the vacant lot across from Arant's, I heard my father grumble. He told us to wait in the car and we watched as he crossed the street and read a note taped to the door. The sun light created a glimmering rainbow with the yellow, red, green, and blue tonic bottles in the window rack. "Arant's on vacation" he said as he turned the ignition switch. In those days the key always stayed in the car. We wound back through the hot dusty streets. I was disappointed, not for the lack of a haircut - it always made my head itch. I missed the gumball machine.

Minutes later the lumbering Studebaker slowed. "We'll stop here, boys" he said as my father turned the big green station wagon into a driveway. I saw a barber pole with its eternal red and blue corkscrew turning on the front of a white painted brick building. A sign posted by the door under the pole said "Men's Haircuts $1, Boy's 85 cents." I'm not sure why the inflated price didn't matter. But never did I think my father was so determined for us to get a trim.

The gravel lot crunched under our shoes. As we entered I noticed the vinyl and chrome chairs seemed shinier than Arant's. The floor was a gleaming black and white checkerboard. The smell of Butchwax was in the air along with the buzz of electric clippers. An array of clippers, their long black cords dangling like hangman's nooses nearly to the floor, was hanging on the wall beside the huge barber mirror. Like Arant's, the mirror made the shop twice as big. But Arant's had a sense of infinite space because from my father's knee level rose massive plate glass windows where the tonic racks ran the length of the bottom edge.

This shop was small. With two chairs like Arant's, but also only one barber. It seemed newer, but it was new to me, so it may have been just as old. I didn't like the absence of big windows. I had been used to the barber shop offering a window to the world, especially from the high vantage point of the chair. The windows here were up high and covered with Venetian blinds. A steel rack filled with old hunting and fishing magazines stood under a window. I didn't see any baseball magazines like Arant kept on a table. My father merely nodded as the barber acknowledged our entrance. I looked at pictures of big fish while we waited.

Like Jonah in the whale, I was absorbed in a large mouth bass with a big hook snagged through his gills, when the barber's voice rang out "Which one of you boys will be first?" He was finishing a customer, an old man in a red plaid flannel shirt, which seemed inappropriate on this warm day. He shut off the electric clippers and as he turned to hang them on the wall rack, I noticed the crutches supporting the barber. I was attuned to the leg injuries of baseball players. Mantle was hobbled many times in his career and I once saw a player leave a game after sliding into second. His pants were torn and blood oozed through the gash. And football players sometimes stood on the side lines, helmet in hand, propped up on crutches. But much to my horror, as the barber maneuvered from behind the chair, it wasn't an injury to his leg. There was no leg at all.

I turned cold and clammy. The barber fumbled through jars and combs on his table and then drew out a straight razor. He slapped it back and forth on a leather strap hanging from the chair. Behind the strap dangled his pants leg, neatly folded and joined with safety pins. As he lathered the old man's neck, I vaguely recalled that my father had first responded to the barber something about "Cut the young boy first." Me.

I had seen an old colored man in downtown Birmingham rolling around in a "Radio Flyer" wagon. He had no legs. Between war stories and railroad accidents, since my father had labored in both, I had learned that a man could lose a leg.

"Hold on, Mr. Gardner" the barber requested, as he placed the corner of a towel on the old man's neck with his finger. "I have a styptic pencil around here someplace." He fumbled around again on the table, swaying gently on the tripod created by his two crutches and one leg. Crimson blood seeped into the white towel.

I felt my knees quake and that twitching feeling around the eyes that every boy knows from holding back tears. One slip of the straight razor and you could lose a leg.

The barber was now wiping off the old man's neck. The sharp red line could be clearly seen. He then pulled out a long pointed pair of scissors and began pruning the old man's ear. "Ouch" the old man flinched. "Dull shears: the barber muttered. "They don't cut clean."

I watched his folded pants leg sway as he moved behind the chair. "Cut clean" I muttered in my mind. My eyes fought through the tears. They cut back and forth, zigzagging from the electric clippers on the wall to the straight razor on the table to the dull shears now trimming the old man's eye brows.

It would be only seconds until it was time to "cut the young boy first." I was afraid my quivering would attract my father's attention. Didn't want him to see me cry. Never.

The old man sprang from the chair to pay for his haircut. While watching the barber maneuver on his tripod to the cash drawer, I saw the seat board leaning against the counter. The perfect guillotine for a little boy's leg.

My knees shook beneath the stiff folds of my jeans. The lump in my throat felt as though I swallowed a jelly bean sideways. My father had little patience for not following through on the order of the day. I felt almost a patriot in accepting my sentence. Character could be built, even on deconstructed limbs - I supposed.

My whole body shivered as though the shop had turned into a walk-in freezer. Like the one at the grocery store where the butcher would disappear to find a special cut of meat my mother wanted. A butcher that didn't have all his fingers.

I slowly climbed up the footrest, the seat, and onto the board the barber placed across the arms. Like climbing a scaffold to an execution. I couldn't hold back the tears any longer. It didn't constrain me that Mickey Mantle never cried. The buzz of the electric clipper as it landed on the back of my neck broke through my soul as easy as my father's swing blade cut through the honeysuckle on the back fence.

A boy died that day. Would it have been a primitive rite of passage, a man would have been born. Just a boy's death. Through the tears I saw the blurred world of my father, my brother, the rack of hunting and fishing magazines, and a couple of old men sitting on the vinyl and chrome chairs.

The world from the back window of the Studebaker was a dull gray. Clouds, sky, houses, trees, all a uniform sameness. No one spoke. A prickly silence. I brushed at the back of my neck to wipe off the itchy clippings. And I rolled up my shirt sleeve to hide the wet spot where I had wiped my face.

perry neel

**Spirit**


Phil stood back to get a street perspective on the new sign in front of the Gardenville Presbyterian Church. "A little to the right" he called to the sexton, Bud. "Ya suh" he shouted back in a servile tone that embarrassed Phil. It seemed too much a throwback to the old south having an illiterate old black man doing the church's custodial work. Once an elder told Phil that Bud had dug graves and rang the church bell for years at a church in Martinsboro. Phil wondered if he also had to stand in the aisle and fan the ladies during service.

"That ought to do it, Bud" said Phil. 'Aw right" chimed Bud as his shuffled on his gimpy legs into the education building to continue mopping the floors. Though old as Methuselah, Bud seemed to get everything done. He was slow but steady. Phil wondered if he was mildly retarded, shy, or just didn't have much to say. Bud was always cheerful, but in the six months he had worked there Phil had never heard him say anything other than "aw right" and "ya suh". He nodded and grinned a lot. It seemed to be enough to communicate everything.

Phil walked up to the sign and opened its glass front. He reached in to adjust the middle initial of his name: Philip E. Mann. "Looks good Phil" a voice called across the church yard from the parking lot. Edward, a close associate from a neighboring town strolled across the scorched grass in the August heat. Sweat rolled down his forehead as he lifted a white straw hat to wipe his brow with a blue bandana. "What brings you to town?" Phil inquired.

"Oh, just needed a little computer paper. And to get the hell out of Nottingham for a while."

"I know what you mean" Phil added.

"Being the preacher is like being a fire plug. You spend half your time putting out fires and the other half getting pissed on."

"Ain't it the truth" Phil agreed.

With a pat on the back, Phil asked Edward to join him for lunch if he had the time. "Always have time" he replied. They walked down a block from the church and picked up some sandwiches and cold drinks at the diner and took them back to Phil's office. "Damn, that corner at Main and 3$^{rd}$ is the hottest place I've ever seen. Always five degrees hotter than anywhere else. Did you see the bank thermometer – said 101."

"Sit here and cool off a while" Phil offered, "I've got nothing on schedule for this afternoon."

Phil and Edward enjoyed their lunch, sharing gossip about local clergy and griping about their congregations. Edward was a bit unconventional as far as clergy go. He was a bright seminarian but struggled with his faith and had trouble with the expectations country people had for "the preacher". His scraggly hair, jeans, and straw hat did not fit the picture... any more than his radical views. Phil, by all appearances, through to his button down blue oxford shirt and khaki pants, was all a good Virginia Presbyterian should be. Hampden-Sydney College and Union Seminary. He had the ideal family of a wife who worked at home, a daughter and a son.

And a family dog. His sermons always brought smiles and handshakes and the occasional pat on the back. Contrarily, Edward was always in hot water with his elders and preached sermons that made people shake their heads. Though opposites in many ways, Phil and Edward were drawn to each other as sojourners. Edward was constantly on the move, tracking down God like a Southside Virginia deer dog. His journey was visible in his constant movement and his rambling talk. Phil's journey was inward, silent, and not apparent at all to those around him. Phil read constantly. World religions, psychology, spirituality. He privately wrote poems that detailed his journey, of pitfalls and losing his way.

"If it weren't for the people, the church would be a good place to work" Phil observed wryly, knowing this unorthodox statement would ring a bell with Edward.

"Damn straight" he replied.

A creak sounded and Bud inched open the door, sticking his head in as though expecting to find trouble. "Come in Bud" Phil invited. "Ya suh", his customary reply as he gently lifted the waste paper can and carried it outside the office to empty. His handling of the can reminded Phil of news clips of the police removing terrorist bombs. One slight mishap and it's over. Phil chuckled to himself realizing the only bombs that waste basket contained were old sermons.

"Still hot out there?" Edward asked in the old southern tradition of talking about the obvious being better than not talking at all. "Ya suh" was Bud's response as he shuffled out.

"Doesn't say much, does he?" Edward asked.

"Might as well simplify it to numbers- 1 and 2," Phil explained.

"What do you mean?"

"He's been here six months and I've only heard him say two things – 'aw right' and 'ya suh'. He could save himself trouble and just say 'one' or 'two'. They sat bemused a second, then a volley of laughs.

"Well, I guess he has life figured out," Edward suggested.

"Huh".

"Just seems we spend all our time trying to figure out how to say things. Either to say what we mean or to say something that doesn't sound like what we mean."

"I guess so."

"Sure. Think about it. We've both been to college and seminary. You are a language scholar, Phil, and I can put "DR." in front of my name. What do we know that Bud doesn't know?"

"I don't know, Edward. He doesn't say much but what I told you. I think he's mildly retarded. I do know he drinks a little bit on pay day, so maybe the drinking has dulled his mind."

"No Phil, you miss my point. It is not how much you know. It's just whether you know the things you need to know. Our heads are crammed full of mostly worthless stuff. Why can't we reduce it to only the essentials."

"I wish that were possible." Phil pondered the thought. "You may be right about Bud. He's not suffering. He may seem poor to us, but he has everything he needs. I've heard the house where he rooms is decent. He works part time here and part time at Hardees' as a janitor. Has no immediate family, but a niece who checks on him now and then. Other than a little limp, he seems healthy enough. Never misses a day."

"Yeah, and he has the good sense to enjoy himself a little on payday. That's more than you or I ever do," Edward noted.

After a pause, Phil observed "Have you noticed, even on these hot, Southside Virginia days, Bud never sweats?"

"O Lord, that's it. We've finally found a true Christian. I'm convinced."

About that time the door cracked open again as the top of Bud's boney head appeared through the opening. He leaned in, never actually placing his feet in the office. Always a line of demarcation where Bud kept to his own side. He had changed clothes, his shirt was a corny looking plaid, the type that made fast food workers appear to be mindless fools. A big streak of grease was smeared across his shoulder down toward his chest. Maybe where he cradled the mop handle. The name tag was smudged so that only part of Bud's last name was legible. It said "Bud Ha" instead of "Bud Harmon." Phil thought the burger joint could at least supply enough clean uniforms.

"Your check is on the secretary's desk, Bud" Phil said. Bud nodded and closed the door, his day at the church done. "Every Friday it's the same. He doesn't speak, just pokes his head in the door, gets his check, goes down to the shopping center to mop greasy floors, buys a bottle of wine at Piggly Wiggly and no one sees him till Monday."

"I'd trade for that," Edward offered. "Would simplify my life. No hard decisions. No people to keep happy. None of the BS that you and I put up with – Presbyteries, church sessions, local politics, even family."

"Sounds like giving up a lot of responsibility to me?' Phil questioned.

"Sure is.  Responsibility that most of the time we shouldn't take. Responsibility is power and too many people have power over too much.  If each one of us could reduce our lives down to the bare minimum, like Bud, then we wouldn't have all the problems we have – personal, social, political, environmental – you name it.  All problems are issues of power, and until we can have power over our own lives, and not others,  nothing will change for the better."

"So, if I want to change my life and thus change the world I should…" Phil trailed off his sentence with the wave of his hand, wanting Edward to complete the thought.

"You should quit all this theology and self-help crap and look at someone like Bud, and do like him."

Phil broke out in laughter.  "You're kidding?"

"No I'm not."

"Sure."

"You put up your books and watch Bud."

"As though Bud were Thoreau, or Jesus Christ, for heaven's sake!  I haven't seen you do it."

"It's too scary."

"What do you mean?"

"I might actually have to be responsible for myself, and that's scary.  Besides, I don't know what I'm talking about.  None of us can be responsible for ourselves.  And even if old Bud has got it down, it's just an accident.  Good luck.  Hell, grace I should say. You can't make it happen.  Isn't it the spirit?  That's what we are supposed to believe."

"Grace.  Spirit…"  Phil mumbled to himself.

-------------------------------------------

Rap, rap, rap.  The old wooden screen door bounced off the door frame with each knock.  A shuffle came from the dark room.  The only light seemed to come from the back somewhere.  Possibly a kitchen.

"Ya suh" was the eventual response.

"It's Rev. Mann," the caller answered.  "Uh, Phil."

He adjusted the paper sack under his arm.  A long green bottle neck protruded from the sack.

The screen door creaked open as a long black arm pushed it out. The spring made an almost musical clinging sound as it stretched open.  Phil stepped into the dark room and stood silently.

"Aw right."

perry neel

## Simon and Loretta

"On one occasion," the old man went on, "Simon was sitting in the front seat of their car while Loretta went into a store downtown." The old man stopped to stick a finger in his ear. I didn't think his ear really itched because he appeared to be stimulating his brain instead.

"Yep. Simon was pretty worthless, but the women would do anything for him. He just sat there smoking a Chesterfield while she went looking for him a new pair of shoes. She wanted her man to look sharp at the dance hall on Saturday night."

The storyteller took a gulp from his Old Milwaukee and pondered the sequence of events. I eased back in the booth, well aware how these stories can drag on. Reached in my shirt pocket for a cigarette and a book of matches.

"And Simon could dance. Many a young gal lost her virginity dancing with him." He let out a sinister chuckle. "Damn nears, anyway..." I pondered the changes in the ways men and women now understand each other. This old guy still found amusement in how men were supposed to be rough pedagogues of the facts of life, as though a woman never learned unless a man forced the issue. I wondered if he realized anything had changed.

"Loretta. She woulda' sold her soul for Simon. Of course she didn't know she could stand in the front of the line. And she didn't have to do much of nothin', either. Simon was ahead of his time. This was long before them pretty boys like James Dean and Elvis. Real men were cowboys, or so we thought. You had to be tough. A loner. But oh how them women loved a man to take care of. Most of us guys were too stupid to see it. We wanted to be like John Wayne or Humphrey Bogart. Anyway, she bought him them shoes, two-tone black and white. And when they showed up at the dance that Saturday, Simon in them two-tone shoes, blue jeans with cuffs in 'em and white shirt with the sleeves rolled up, I'd a thought half the boys in town woulda taken him outside and whooped his ass. Man, they hated this guy. But most of them didn't want to mess up their suits. I suspect they were afraid he'd mess up their faces."

I sipped from my beer, not sure any longer of the point of this story, but I had heard so many over my years of hanging out at this beer joint. Me being the young, outa place, professional guy among blue collar men. But I grew up in one of these, so it felt familiar. My father, the railroad engineer took me every morning when he got home from work. His happy hour, I guess. At first, I liked hearing the stories of these old men, but after a while they were as bland as the brown tile floor. But the old guys liked to talk, and I felt a tribal obligation to hear them out.

To my surprise, the old man jumped up from his seat. "Gotta put some George Jones on the jukebox." Sometimes I felt that the men in this place had to tell stories just to fill the silence. It was a wonder he was aware the music had stopped. I hadn't.

"Dance? Lord that Simon could dance. He could glide any woman across the floor like she was on oil, but Loretta, she was floatin' on ball bearings. All the boys looked like crows lined up on a wire, standing there in them dark suits with neckties hangin' like their tongues a droolin'. They weren't loud, but they were squawkin'. How could this big city boy roll into town without no job and all the women gather round him like some harem? Loretta never took her eyes off his. And those two-tone shoes!"

"What's with the shoes?" I thought. I hoped there would be a point to the story

As if he had read the question from my mind, the old man continued. "It was the shoes that started all the trouble. Ole Bobby Hartsfield already resented Simon 'cause he, Bobby, had dated Loretta and even though she already dumped him, he kept his claim on her. Bobby worked down at the grocery store and his family was pretty poor. He knew his old jalopy wouldn't attract no girls, but when he saw Simon that day layin' back in the front seat of Loretta's Oldsmobile, the one her daddy bought her, smokin a cigarette, he nearly flipped. Of course, he hadn't got over it by Saturday night. Well, Simon went outside for a smoke and was leanin' up against a lamp post. Bobby and a bunch of his friends come out to stir up some trouble. 'Where'd you get them pretty boy shoes?' he asked. Now since he was already sportin' a grudge, you can imagine when Simon told him 'Loretta bought 'em…' First thing Bobby did was kick dirt on those shoes and then he started to take off his coat for a fight. But by the time he pulled off his coat and tie Simon was bent over untying his shoes. Bobby didn't know what to do. Simon slipped them off, dusted 'em with his sleeve and held 'em out to Bobby. "Looks like they'll fit." He stuck them in Bobby's hand and flicked his cigarette down on the gravel and walked off in his sock feet. Last anybody ever saw him, Simon was crossing the street. Can you believe it, in his sock feet."

The old man paused. I guessed it was the end of the story. He stood up as George Jones wound down on the jukebox. Then, reaching in his shirt pocket, he fished out some ones and said, "I'll buy your beer." He flopped them out on the table, and a bill slid off the edge onto the floor. I looked up and said "Thanks." As I reached down to pick it up, I spotted his battered old two-tone shoes. "Don't mention it," he said, and he walked out the screen door.

## Waffle House

The sizzle on the grill could not match my frying forehead as I wiped the sweat from my brow with my wrist. My grip on the ballpoint pen clamped down like a lobster claw as I ran through yet another chorus of the options that go along with a western omelet. Never mind if the customer can read, he will always want me to say it. Lazy, illiterate, the reason didn't matter to me. Customers are stupid, that's all! One more late-night shift in this hell hole was a hundred more than I ever wanted to spend. "Hash browns or home fries?" I didn't know whether I'd shove them in his ear or down his throat. Whoever thought of two ways to fry potatoes anyway?

As I turned to relay the order to the self-described genius who happened to double as a short order cook, I felt that twinge in my belly. Simultaneous urges of maternal warmth and retching. "Ten months pregnant," I always said to the customers who asked. I really felt like saying "I'm only fat." Why I avoided the cruelty I don't know. Maybe I wasn't sure if it was being cruel to them or me.

"I hate this fucking place," I muttered as I handed the ticket to Tesla the Grillmaster. And out the back door holding my stomach. I leaned against the fender of my old Ford Fairlane and tried to throw up. The pain became sharper, but I could only gag. The 3 a.m. air felt cool to my cheeks. I breathed deeply and slowly. Gravel crunched under my shoes as I paced around the car. I wanted to drive off in the dark and never look back. Instead, I adjusted the apron so I wouldn't feel so bound. If only this baby would come. Just two weeks early. That's all I ask. Then I could quit this damned place. But I knew that as long as I could stand, I had to work. Here I was, eighteen and pregnant. I still remember those glowing words of my high school guidance counselor, "Layne, you have such promise. Don't blow it." Promise blown.

Randell was the cook who doubled as night manager. It was a goofy name the way he said it. "Ran Dell," in two distinct syllables. Claimed he once studied physics and planned to teach it someday. He gave me one of his double message looks as I brushed between him and the counter. At my size, I brushed into everything. I could never tell if he wanted me to see his displeasure with my work, or if he was trying to show sympathy. Managerial training course graduate, so who knows. Since he hadn't fired me, I took it as sympathy. "Order up," he squealed in his redneck high pitch. Physics teacher. Really good career moves, I figured. Maybe prison. "Blown promise. Indeed" I snickered to myself.

I put down the plates for the couple in the corner booth. Poured black coffee. The two lovebirds didn't notice. If they were so interested in each other, why were they here? Why was anyone here? What do people do so that they need a restaurant in the middle of the night? I wanted to cry.

"Layne," the state trooper called as he nodded and slipped a dollar bill under his coffee cup. The cop was one of the few nice people who ever came in here. He let me go once when he caught me speeding. I was late to class at the community college. There was a joint closed up in the ashtray. A class I dropped because pregnancy, work, and school weren't working out. The joint is still in the ashtray.

I snapped up the dollar and went over to the coffee maker to start a fresh pot. Melody, the other waitress on late night was leaning against the counter smoking a cigarette. She was pretty worthless, but at least didn't mind this dreadful job. She would have been the "happy doing anything" type. But she sometimes was a little too friendly with some of the idiots that came in here. Melody was a sucker for the line "I can't talk to my wife like I can talk to you."

I grit my teeth in hopes she wouldn't say something about some man. Men, who the hell needs them? It was a goddamned pizza delivery boy who couldn't understand that delivering his son was the most important job he had undertaken is his short miserable life. Now he's in Florida holed up with some crackhead.

"Layne, check out the biker dude," she whispered. A middle aged guy in a leather jacket took a seat. "My station" I whispered back while I lumbered over to this tattooed Santa Claus dressed in black. I needed tips. All a guy had to do was wander in here in the middle of the night and state "I am a jerk" and Melody would be loosening the top button of her blouse. Sometimes I felt like I was the only thing saving her from misery worse than mine.

"How you, honey?" he beamed through a row of gold capped teeth. It was all I could do to keep from pouring the whole steaming pot of coffee in his lap. My cold stare meant business and he ordered his food without incident. It was so hot my uniform stuck to my back. The grill sizzled and my life in hell continued.

The clock ground toward 4. I grabbed a towel to wipe the counter. The biker had been nursing his coffee and I felt the whole time like he was watching me nude.

"How'd you like me to come back and pick you up when you get off?" He fished the chain wallet from his hip pocket. "Do I look like I want to go out with you or anybody else?!" I leaned over the counter right in his wooly face, certain he could feel the flames leap off my cheeks.

"Why honey, can't blame a man for trying." He threw down a ten and left without waiting for change. I would have thrown it in his face.

"You meet all the requirements," Melody smiled. Puzzled, I looked at her but before I could speak, she interrupted. "A biker don't look for much. Just a woman who'd stay up all night. And one who would have sex..."

"What?"

"Look, its 4 in the morning. And from the looks of you, you've had sex at least once before. That's all you need, baby."

"Great! What about tattoos? I don't have any."

"They are just gravy. It's a good addition to any meal, but don't need it to eat." Could I sink any lower? Pregnant, miserable, no future. And attractive to aging bikers.

It was 6 o'clock before I knew it. Nice to slide into my jeans, especially with that expandable baby section in the front. I sat on a crate in the stock room and rubbed my feet. Melody clicked across the floor in a pair of black spiked heels. She slipped her thin arms into a sequined jacket. I never asked why a woman would dress like that at 6 in the morning. I didn't want to know. I didn't care what other women did. Her feet left little tracks on the powdered tile where someone, Randell probably, spilled waffle mix. A cold blast of air hit me as the door slammed behind Melody. "Later, hon," she shouted over her shoulder. Moments later, I trudged through the door and onto the thick gravel which had a light coat of frost on it.

I slid onto the seat, thankful for an old car with bench seats. Stuck in the key and the dashboard lit faintly. The horizon was beginning to lighten. I felt the baby move as I fastened the safety belt around my bulging stomach. I wanted a cigarette, but pulled a stick of Juicy Fruit out of my bag. In the rear view mirror I could see the billow of exhaust. A florescent tube in the "Waffle House" sign flickered in the shifting light. I pointed the Fairlane out of the back lot and left behind a life so real for yet another one.

perry neel

## Communion

The communion cup felt lighter this time. The Altar Guild had gone to the cheap disposable cups instead of the heavy "shot" glasses we had all grown up with. In the interest of sanitation in this day of AIDS and other germs the guild insisted that people were staying away from communion. The church was now "open to homosexuals and street people, and whatever other undesirables we can dig up." Not my thoughts, just something of a litany among the parish complainers. My concern had been more over the fact that the plastic cups are not bio-degradable. "People's health should come first" was the resounding chorus of the Altar Guild. I conceded, as any parish minister would.

I was glad the Elder serving me did not stand there and wait for me to throw it down like a Texas cowboy in a saloon. Some of them do. But it's not cheap bourbon. It is "the new covenant written in my blood." I like a little time for reflection, to at least give the somber appearance of prayerful piety. After all, I am up front and everyone can see me.

Welch's grape juice. I detest it. Would Jesus have served potato chips if they had them? Most of the older folks remember the days of homemade communion wine. This is a country church. The good times of the wine-makers and friends must have been far greater than the present sober fellowship at the Lord's Table. The silver trays, the plastic cups, the android Elders stalking up and down the sanctuary surely bear no resemblance to the farewell meal of Jesus. He and his friends just sitting around a table. They may have talked about the weather and politics. Sports. In somebody's kitchen. And if the juice of the grape didn't pack a little punch, I'm sure they would have sent it back! I imagine Peter would.

The organ droned, casting a spell which suited the mood. Jesus is dead alright. Probably glad, too, if he could see this charade. I picked a piece of stale crust from between my teeth. Time to wash down the Wonder Bread with some ersatz blood. Down the hatch. And then I waited.

It took twice as long for the Elders to make their rounds with the cups than with the bread. The parishioners were slower, taking care not to spill the grape juice on their nice clothes. I find it a good time to be repentant of my irreverence. To wish I had the faith of the pious on the back row. Or the faith of the Elders who so sincerely bear the pall. But today my heart has little capacity for suffering. Strangely, it is love that distracts me from the holy. Love, erotic and sensual. Love that has no place in the church, forbidden from the clergy.

I long to undress her. To feel her warm, shimmering skin against mine. To grab her with such force, cling to her in great weakness. To make love to her and fall asleep at her breast. I see the blue of her eyes, brighter and more pure than the stained glass. I feel the wetness of her sweat, baptizing me from head to toe, making me whole.

"Crack." I felt the plastic splinter between my clutched hands. A warm wetness rolled down between my fingers and the blood started to drip from my right hand onto my satin stole and black clerical robe. I opened my palm where the fractured cup is set in a pool of blood. I reached with my left hand to remove the splinter and felt a prick. A shard hung in the palm of my left hand. Quickly I gathered the pieces of the cup and placed them on the crumb covered bulletin and put it on the seat beside me. I took the green stole and wiped my hands, the blood staining the simple embroidered Latin cross. A crimson streak ran down the satin until it was caught in the gold fringe.

I was not aware of anything else until the organ stopped. The Elders were poised for their return to the table. After they were seated, I served them. Then, I opened the crumbed and stained bulletin which held the plastic pieces, to lead the closing prayer. We all said the words "We thank you Lord for your great Love..."

perry neel

## Frog Hunting

We used to go out with flashlights at night, my brother Tommy and me. It was on hot summer nights, filled with mosquitoes and heat lightning. We'd go to our little backyard oasis under the fig tree. The metal case of an expired hot water tank, turned on its side, halved. The oasis was filled with murky greenish water, the sides hairy with algae. Rock castles we had stacked up after scouring the yard for building materials towered from the dim depths below to majestic heights above the surface. Fish could hide when birds would come to drink and bathe. Sometimes we could catch a glimpse, a glimmer from a fantail. Sometimes the goldfish hovered like submarines, suddenly to dart into our makeshift caverns at the awareness of a catbird or boy-child gods peering down from the heavens, through the darkness of night and water.

But on these nights, it was not goldfish that prompted our search. Cheap nickel goldfish. They commanded only brief admiration, and most often ended floating side-up, waiting for a quick but solemn burial or to serve as lunch for a catbird or robin. Those nights we were in search of the ancient beast, from a time before time, the constant and unchanging since the realm of the dinosaurs. The bullfrog. It was a grand search. Fearsome, ineffable, godlike, we were in awe just at his prospect. His bulging omniscient eyes, his powerful legs that could take him to foreign lands in a tremendous hop, his darting, devouring tongue. Like God, we could never touch him. Too elusive. Too fast. Even if one could lay a hand on him, how would he feel? Does he really inflict a plague of warts?

Many nights we would go out and search for God. Most nights searching in vain. Sometimes his evidence was overwhelming. His night rending croak. The splash like an Acapulco diver into the pond. We knew he was there. But we seldom set eyes on him. His life shrouded in holy mystery.

But then there were nights, in the spotlight of our version of an acolyte's candle, the trusty Eveready flashlight, he would sit and gloat over his kingdom in plain sight. A testimony of his accessibility, his mundane ordinariness. His majesty. Lord over his kingdom. But we dare not touch God. Ridiculous, we were. On those nights we thought we would frighten him!

One night I went out alone. Pajama clad. There was a slight chill, even on this August night. I had to shake the Eveready to goad it into shining. I had been lured all evening by his beckoning. The call through the windows of our den. I was possessed by an unfounded confidence, youth mistaking itself for maturity. I knew the frog would be there. I would see him. I would touch him. Tonight.

I surveyed the rock edges of the pond with my golden beam. All was silent. He had stopped calling me. Maybe he had gone away. I searched through the shoots of the fig tree overhanging the pond. Lifting fuzzy leaves, pushing back springy brances. I began to doubt my search. I gazed back toward the house, fearful my brother would come out. He would surely scare him away. I alone had been called, like Isaiah in our Sunday School lesson. Boxes of light shined out from the windows, but only half-way out into the yard. I stood alone in faith. In shadow. In darkness with no moon.

I probed with the light down into the depths of the water. Often he must have hidden there. If he was, I would surely fail my quest. The rocks and shadows were a thousand hiding places. Rocks and fallen figs and fish floating in stillness.

My light combed the ground around the pond and under the tree. Quickly I doubled back. A penny? What was that circle that flashed in the sweep of my light? At least I might turn a profit! I swung the light back and captured a bright circle, a flash of gold, then two. Two cents? No. The eyes of God.

The frog was frozen there on a clean patch of dirt. His stony presence was as much a tombstone or memorial than an incarnation. Was he real? Had I found him too late? He just sat in solid stillness.

Slowly I bent down. I could feel my pajama legs inch up my calves. I stretched out my hand. It shook. The cold night air or my being so bold as to try and touch the divine? Would I find him... dead? My trembling finger came down slowly. Finally to rest on the top of his head. The eyes were unmoving. Caught between the euphoria of a completed pilgrimage and the dread of commiting sacrilege, I kept my finger on his head. He felt neither cold nor warm. Wet nor dry. I had the feeling that my finger and his head were one continuous thing.

Since one can stand only so long at a shrine, or in the awe of the holy, after a moment, I stood up slowly, my finger still extended with wonder.

As I stood, the flashlight fluttered, but in its dimming light I saw movement. A plop and a splash on my ankle. I turned off the light and walked barefoot to the house. I said nothing and went in silence to my room. It had all been so simple. But what had it been? Was it my search, my will to track him down? Or was it his way of being generous with me? I stared at the ceiling from my bed and wondered where he had gone.

## Echo Man

The lightness of the spring air gave buoyancy to the voices of the people on Main Street. The college women and prep-schoolers were out in large numbers, reveling in the first warm days of the year and spending their parents' money to the delight of the town merchants. Wynton betrayed the myth of the dying small town in America. Sure, there were problems, but on the whole the town fared better than most. A lot of businesses had been lost to the mall. But some old ones stuck it out and survived. And became revered as town icons to be venerated. New ones also opened up on occasion. So the town was far from stagnant.

There were other reasons Wynton wouldn't die. Being a regional hub for state institutions, it was home for many state employees. The mental hospital and the prison were the largest. And since mental illness and crime were not likely to go out of business, jobs were secure. There was also the tiny women's college and the Episcopal School.

Daniel had grown a reluctant appreciation for Wynton. In many ways it embodied the kind of narrow, deep seated conservatism he had fought all his life. But he eventually succumbed over the four years he resided there to the tranquility of what was rapidly being lost in America: small town life. After all, it was rural but not really a farming community. It had industry, but the air and water were clean. Higher education and culture were in disproportionate abundance compared to other towns its size. Crime was low. The little college where he worked and the Episcopal Church he attended sat high up on the hill shining their dual beams of guiding light upon the town. It dawned on him that the fervor and intensity of city life, he had mistaken for passion. Approaching middle age, this setting was ample for the kind of reassessments he'd been working on. Like one is often surprised while decorating for a party or a holiday, things are ready before you think they are done. You don't need all the other stuff and put it back in the closet.

Daniel nodded to a few familiar faces as he strolled down Main Street toward the diner. While Wynton was slow to accept newcomers as its own, it never fell short of playing fully the southern role of kindness.

"So good to see you, Daniel," Mrs. Ball chimed as they passed. "I hope your family is well." His wife and two girls.

"Why thank you, they are, Mrs. Ball." He half turned as they passed so his words would not miss her half deaf ear. An abrupt bump caused him to turn back in surprise. "Pardon me," his automatic response. To which the short, dark haired man answered in like manner. Something seemed odd about the man. His hair was short but uncombed. His plaid flannel shirt oddly paired with a striped necktie. The blue pants were too short, exposing institutional shoes. Sometimes Daniel did not recognize many of the former mental health patients now turned loose to live freely on the streets. Many were passable as eccentric citizens. A few were alcoholics panhandling for money. And there was the usual assortment of mumblers walking around, staring at the ground as though treasure might appear underfoot. "Bums" his parents would have called them. But Daniel's liberal education had crowned them with a less ominous title, "de-institutionalized persons." Or the common, yet incongruously happy sounding "street people." Lumped in there with "street performer," "street musician," "street magician."

Turning through the double oak doors of the diner, Daniel took his customary table at the bay window. He nodded to the waitress, "The usual," and unfolded the daily paper and placed it on top of his file folder of lecture notes. Teaching philosophy at the college was a job he had taken seriously over his four years in Wynton. Full time opportunities were slim with all the budget cutbacks in higher education. He worked hard hoping to make tenure. Yet recently he started to back off the intensity and settle into a more graceful southern life. Coffee and toast at the diner on Main while looking over the local paper now seemed as important as extra time in a library carrel or working for some social justice cause in the community. Fervent scholarship, progressive causes, and even family life all seemed to mellow as though this archaic Dixie paradise had persuaded him to live slowly, calmly, like willow branches fanning out in the afternoon breeze.

He nodded to the assorted regulars at the diner. Old men, the old mafia of Wynton. Young men, the new elite. Tourists. Students. Daniel felt at ease in this point of life. Alive for once without the stifling demands of progress and success.

He smiled as the waitress poured the coffee, although he

struggled to remember her name.  So he dare not try and be mistaken.  Behind her he caught a glimpse of a man slipping through the doors and walking up to the checkout counter.  It was the funny little man he bumped on the street.  Comical in his mismatched attire. He stood rocking gently back and forth on one foot.  Like he was trying to push a nail in the floor that had worked its way up.

The other waitress, Hannah, he remembered her name, pushed a ticket down on the spike next to the cash register and looked up at the man.  Her expression wore fatigue and boredom.  Daniel did not like that expression, for it questioned the acceptance of this virtuous life.  The man merely gazed blankly at Hannah.

"Well, what do you want?"  It was as much snarl as question. "Well, what do you want?" the man replied.

Puzzled, the waitress looked hard at the man, but before she could speak, Daniel's waitress stepped in and resolved the dilemma. "Coffee, two creams, two sugars."   "Coffee, two creams, two sugars," the man repeated.  Hannah walked back to kitchen and returned with styrofoam cup and mashed a plastic lid tight down on it. "A dollar and five cent," she demanded.  Daniel hated the local confusion regarding money and the apparent inability to distinguish how to regard it as a noun or an adjective.

"A dollar and five cent," the man mimicked.  He pulled the money out of a pocket stuffed with a handkerchief, pocket knife, assorted papers, a plastic toy soldier, wrappers, and candy.

Daniel was amused but perplexed by the whole transaction.  It reminded him of singing in rounds in church camp when he was a boy.  Or when he was in France doing research.  His conversational

French being inadequate, he spent much of the time repeating back what the people said to him.

He folded his newspaper and placed it to the side. Picked up his lecture notes and wondered about his students. Academic life for most of them consisted in cloned lecture statements, mirrored textbook responses, and of course, downright internet plagiarism. It wasn't that Daniel looked for originality in his students, rather he wanted thoughtfulness. As he read his lecture, he heard the echoes of students in their essays. He was irritated by the thought that he did not inspire his students in the ways his professors had inspired him.

He gathered his things and paid his bill and exited. Daniel winced at the diesel fumes from a passing truck. He wiped his eyes and trudged up the hill to campus.

It was two weeks later, maybe less, when Daniel's street corner conversation with Mrs. Hinkle from the Historical Foundation was interrupted by a screech of tires. The motorist then hit the accelerator making the tires squeal again. He stuck his head out the window and pumped his fist, "Get out of the way you sonofabitch!" Scrambling to the curb, the odd man in same plaid shirt and striped tie pumped his fist and yelled back "Get out of the way you sonofabitch!" The man was bleeding from his forearm and cheek. He must have fallen against the concrete. Daniel and Mrs. Hinkle ran over to him. "Are you alright, hon?" she asked.

The man was a bit stunned from his fall. He grabbed a signpost for support. His eyes rolled a bit. Then he turned toward Mrs. Hinkle, "Are you alright, hon?"

perry neel

Mrs. Hinkle was taken aback.  Daniel was amused.  So many times he had mocked southern politeness in his head by repeating the phrases, but never had the nerve to speak.  The man appeared to be ok, but before Daniel was sure, Mrs. Hinkle ushered him away, uttering "...of all the nerve."  Behind them, Daniel heard in a hushed tone, "of all the nerve."

"Echo Man," he named this odd little fellow.  He began to notice him more and more around town.  Always saying back to others what had been said to him.  Sort of a backward conversational version of the golden rule.

One day while drinking coffee at the diner, Daniel saw Echo Man come in to get a cup to go.  Fortunately, the waitress who seemed to know his game brought his coffee without any words being exchanged.  Rather, echoed.  Daniel was standing to pay his bill when the odd fellow turned to leave, almost bumping him again.  At the chance of being friendly, Daniel stuck out his hand and said, "I don't believe we have been introduced.  I'm Daniel."  To which the man replied exactly in kind.  Without so much as a nod, the man left.  For a second Daniel thought they had the same name.  But then caught himself.  The waitress saw the perplexed look on his face. "Oh, he's ok. He just doesn't have anything original to say," and she almost laughed.  Daniel, curious, replied, "But why does he always repeat what is said to him?"  "Gets me," she shrugged indifferently.

A man who only says what is first spoken to him.  Daniel stopped by the office of a colleague who chaired the Psychology Department.  Dr. Reid chuckled.  "Are you looking for a new discipline? Sounds like a good research project to me.  I've never heard of such a thing."

"It just seems so unusual."

"You've got that right," and Reid laughed again. "Echo Man." "Maybe it is more in your department anyway. A philosophical issue... He could be perfectly normal, you know."

Over the weeks Daniel gave regular but passing thought to Echo Man. He did not try to speak to him anymore. By winter, he did not see him as much either.

An early December snow paralyzed Wynton. It caught the ever regular town unprepared. Big ridges of snow lined the streets like low walls. The plows made sure no one could park, filling the curbs and sidewalks. Quickly cabin fever brought out the folks who lived downtown. It was a cheery atmosphere of townies and students, all bonded like Eskimos who'd endured a blizzard.

Taking a break from reading exams, Daniel joined the snowbunnies along Main Street. Felt right for a cup of coffee if the diner was open. He hoped it was and headed that way. What he initially took for the sounds of a snowball fight turned out to be cries for help. He cautiously jogged through the slush toward the scene down the street. "Help." "Help." "Will someone please help him?" "Will someone please help him?"

A woman was crouched down at the street where a flow of melting snow had cut a gap in the plowed ridge. Underneath her was Echo Man, his legs and lower torso dangling beneath a sewer grate that had been dislodged by the city's snow plow. He was clinging to the curb with one arm and the grate with the other. A spilled styrofoam cup of coffee dripped down into the drain mingling with the water that poured over Echo Man and into the sewer main. The woman was clutching him under his armpits, struggling to keep him from falling deeper into the storm sewer.

"He's stuck and I'm afraid I will lose my grip," she pleaded to Daniel.

"He's stuck and I'm afraid I will lose my grip," Echo Man repeated.

"Here, let me get him," Daniel urged as he knelt down and reached his arms around Echo Man's chest from behind him.

"Here, let me get him." He gasped the words, struggling for breath, constricted by Daniel's hold.

But he was too heavy for Daniel to lift. He strained in the freezing cold water. Echo Man was like a heavy sandbag.

"Pull the grate aside and maybe we can lift his legs out so he can support himself," Daniel instructed the woman.

"Pull the grate aside and maybe we can lift his legs out so he can support himself," Echo Man huffed in response.

The woman struggled to move the iron grate. Two men suddenly appeared and helped to drag it aside. They reached down and pulled Echo Man's legs out. After a minute they were able to stand him up. He seemed to be uninjured, but soaked. But he was not shivering like the others. In fact, he appeared nonchalant.

"Are you hurt?" the woman asked. "Are you hurt?" the echo.

It confused the woman. "Yes, I'm fine, but how are you?"

"Yes, I'm fine, but how are you?"

She looked to Daniel. "I don't know," he said. He held up his arms open wide. "He just repeats everything he hears."

"I don't know, he just repeats everything he hears."

"How odd." The woman's look made Daniel wonder if she even cared that she had helped the man. Was she wanting gratitude? Did he not deserve her efforts now that she knew something of the man?

"How odd," Daniel heard from over his shoulder.

He turned toward Echo Man. "You better get home and change into some dry, warm clothes."

"You better get home and change into some dry, warm clothes."

At least that exchange made sense. Daniel was wet and freezing. He walked back up the hill past campus towards home. By the time he reached the top he was nearly stiff from the cold. But he stopped all of a sudden. Turned and looked down the hill at downtown Wynton. He forgot his chill.

The town was a uniform gray. It had a dull sameness. As if the early snow had frozen it in time. But it was not a Currier and Ives scene. The town was already frozen, before the storm. Secure and serene and frozen. Daniel's comfort was shattered. Was this all he could hope for? Does it mean anything at all? Would he ever again call Wynton home? "I don't know" he uttered under his frozen breath. "I don't know?" he repeated. He shuddered. Not from cold but fear. And broke out in shivers. A revelation? Or just his soaked clothes in the wind whipping across the hill.

perry neel

## Airplane

The small plane rolled to a stop less than twenty feet from the penitentiary wall. For a moment the stunned sentries in the watchtower forgot their duties, then finally hit the siren. The Department of Corrections emergency training proved efficient as a black uniformed commando squad deployed with automatic weapons and surrounded the plane. The cockpit door swung open and Grandma surrendered without any resistance.

The six o'clock news team captured her stoic, yet triumphant march to the State Police car. Her demeanor was curious. Part Super Bowl quarterback, part prisoner of war. I didn't know what to expect when she turned her head to the camera. "I'm going to Disney World" or name, rank and serial number.

It all began a year and a half ago at Grandpa's funeral. There was not a dry eye in the place. Except Grandma's. When the family took turns crumbling carnations over the grave, Grandma sent her first, and by no means last, shock wave. Bristly, she marched up to the grave and spit. "There," was all she said. I ran up and grabbed her arm to escort her back to the car. This once gentle old lady jabbed me sharply with her boney elbow right in the ribs. She jumped in the back seat all by herself and slammed the door. Grandma offered no explanation. But I swore I heard her mutter "Good riddance" under her breath as we sped away from the cemetery. The family always said I must have been hearing things. I was certain what I heard. Attributed it all to stress.

After 52 years of marriage, of what appeared to be a happy marriage, it was hard to understand. Then the next week when my wife picked her up from the beauty parlor we were in for another shock. My wife thought the flaming red hair sported by Grandma was some sort of beautician's mishap. She was about to suggest an attorney. Grandma declared, "A red headed woman. Always wanted to be a red headed woman."

That weekend, Mr. Sax down at the supermarket phoned. He said Grandma's car was stuck over a parking barrier in front of the store. I told Mr. Sax he was surely mistaken. He said it was a red Oldsmobile. When I reminded him that Grandpa recently died and that Grandma couldn't drive, he offered that he could not dispute either fact. He suggested I call a tow truck to free the car and bring someone to drive it home. Unless I figured Grandma could drive it home as well.

The whole family tried to persuade Grandma to give up on driving. She didn't want to hear it. Complained all the while about her dependence on others. At last we convinced her that driving school was necessary and that unlike when she was young, these days you had to pass a test to get a license. She found a course for senior citizens but disliked being the only one preparing to take the test for her license. All the others were trying to keep from losing theirs. "Losers," she said. Grandma quit the class and never mentioned it again. My sister showed me the failed written test she found in the wastebasket. Later, Grandma sold the car.

Not all of Grandma's exploits were so ill fated. She managed to persuade her 22 year old neighbor, Jerome Bentley, to take her water skiing. No one ever accused Jerome of good sense. But he swears Grandma twisted his arm. I wondered how a 79 year old woman could manipulate a 22 year old man. Jerome finally took me aside one day and said that Grandma told him she knew what all those tall green plants were that he had been cultivating out behind his garage. He said it wasn't the art of blackmail that threw him so much as her request to roll a joint for her to smoke before getting on the skis. "Said it might calm her nerves. It wasn't enough for mine." Jerome added that you haven't heard anything until you've heard a stoned little old lady "whoopin an hollerin" at 30 miles per hour behind a speedboat.

It all came to a head when Grandma announced one day that she always want to know how to fly. My sister and wife looked at each other. They suppressed their potentially explosive laughter. It was the first I ever heard of it. None of us volunteered. Figured she would forget about it.

Secretly for weeks she got Jerome Bentley to take her out to the county airport. It was Jerome's frantic incoherent call that urged me to turn on channel 4. Something about stealing a plane. The news man was hard to understand because someone behind him was cursing in high volume. Of course, it never occurred to me that in the cockpit of the yellow single engine plane the camera panned to follow was Grandma. Then the reporter said something about a 90 year old and the theft of an airplane. The news van took off in hot pursuit along the highway with the cameraman hanging out the window and the reporter tried to talk while bouncing around in the driver's seat. One hand on the wheel, the other on the mic.

I was swept up in the drama. Whirling past farms and stands of pine trees, the reporter and cameraman were doggedly on the trail of the stolen plane. The plane was low, barely clearing the treetops. Bobbing up and down over trees then pastures. Suddenly up ahead loomed the maximum security prison. "It looks like the plane is going to try to land." The camera zoomed in. Closer, then enough to see into the cockpit. I expected to see an old man. Who steals planes anyway? But this was Bonnie without any Clyde. Now I knew what Jerome was yelling about on the phone. The red hair. That fearless determined look. Grandma was at the stick and heading straight for the big house!

I sat on the floor leaning against the couch as the improbable event unfolded. I feared for her life in vain. Grandma glided in for a flawless landing just outside the prison gates. Then the loud siren. The armed guards. I never thought I would see Grandma gunned down on live TV. The swat team surrounded the plane, and Grandma emerged to stand in triumph on the wing. It didn't help matters when she slapped the hand of the gentlemanly officer who offered to assist her down. But the grinning faces of the guards greatly relieved me. Some couldn't contain their laughter. Their rifles quickly came at rest.

Bursting through the ring of security, the reporter rushed up to her to get some comments as they whisked her away. "What were you doing up there, mam?" An odd sense of respect toward a woman who just hijacked a plane. "Just stretching my wings," she smiled while hopping into the back seat of the patrol car.

**Tao**

I first noticed the change when all the buildings took on the look of cardboard stand ups. The rich architecture I had once admired, now pressed flat. A cardboard village, the kind you see on TV sometimes. Some old geezer filling his basement with model trains and creating cities to go with them. Pixie lands of adult imagination now sprawled out in front of me.

When the doctor wanted to know how the Prozac was working, I told her "I'm a hollow man. I may as well be one of those life size displays of sports heroes they set up to advertise beer at a bar. Not hitting any home runs this way." My appearance might have been convincing of a real man. But I was flat. Without substance. I liked being depressed better. At least then I felt something. Now nothing. Of what value is an indifferent person? A man who takes up space without elbowing it out. Just last week I walked away from some thick necked lout who was trying to flirt with my girl. A real man should have something worth fighting for, shouldn't he? I walked away. "It seems to be controlling the depression, wouldn't you say?" my doctor went on ignoring me. "Sure," was all I could muster in reply. I wrote a $35 check for my co-pay. I knew it would overdraw my account. Then I drove across town to the coffee shop. The needle on the dash read "E".

I was sitting on the same patio at the coffee shop where I used to contemplate the town's splendor. My fine career as a public defense attorney was soaring. I was in love. My senses wide open. I couldn't absorb it all fast enough. Life was French roast. Mysteriously, overnight, something clicked. Or snapped? I don't know. Nothing really happened. Now I looked at the flat surfaces of a decaffeinated world. And I was bland. Sugar? I felt like nothing could perk me up to what I once was.

"Have you checked yesterday's market. The futures?" The soft hand on my shoulder may have gone undetected for a while had a second sense not alerted me. Unaware that I had a future, Rachel's question brought me back into the present.

"Why, no." I was hardly audible. She spoke again before the words got out of my mouth.

"I told my broker that Sentry jumped up to 97 and ½. I almost called you about a sale." She was one of my colleagues in defense. Likes to share investment matters. Has a future. Well planned, apparently. Unlike me. "I see you are taking the day off," Rachel smiled and mashed down the bill of my baseball cap and walked off toward the courthouse. I got up and headed the other direction, leaving half a cup of black decaf on the brown plastic table.

The church bell tolled eleven times, announcing the providence of God all across the town of Everton. I trudged up the hill toward the pleading peal of the chimes, slipping undetected under the watchful omniscience. At the top I turned in through the iron gate into the cemetery. Thought I would walk around one last time. It was a place where I found good company on my recent walks. Dead strangers. I would be joining them soon. It would be nice to be among people who welcomed and understood me. Should I call the office and have the secretary cancel tomorrow's appointments? Go ahead and have them reassigned to another attorney? The silent stones whispered "Shh" in the breeze. I liked an appreciative, assuring audience. Not like judges and juries. A crow cawed overhead, atop the church tower. I craned my head to take in the full 75 feet of brickwork which pointed to sky.

Narrow, arched stained glass windows took up the ground level of the tower. On this side Jesus stood perched on a grassy knoll addressing a crowd of eager disciples. His arms were beckoning. "Come, follow me" must have been the passage. The glass disciples remained frozen. They were not going anywhere. "Come, follow me." The tombstones whispered, "Yesss." A gust whipped up a spiral of leaves in the corner where the tower joined the front of the church. They churned in an upward spiral of red and yellow. The gentle updraft crashed oak and maple into the louvered vents in the tower's second level. Bright red leaves gripped then dripped from the vents, showering down on me. A squirrel shimmied up the rainwater downspout in the corner. In no time he cleared the top and returned to the edge of a notch to peer down at me from the castle fortress cap of the tower. Had he been a medieval archer he could have pierced me with an arrow or drenched me in boiling oil.

I walked over to the corner. Leaves like parchment pelted me, their sharp corners stinging like sleet. I noticed a thick copper ground cable. It ran the entire corner from top to the flower garden at the tower base. Must connect to a lightning rod. I pulled it and with it gave a dull twang as it snapped back. I wondered how many times lightning ever ran from God's fingertip down this wire, safely into the earth. Or were there uncaptured bolts hurled by Zeus, in angry attack against us all, frail earthlings that we are. I twanged the cable again, looped my fingers around it and pulled myself up off my feet. The wire was stout. It could hold my weight. The copper was tarnished a bit which probably would give me greater purchase. I needed only to pull up over the stained glass so that I could dig a toe into the louvered vents. Then use them like a ladder, Jacob's ladder. The cable dug into my palms as I gripped tighter for the hard pull. I put one foot on the window ledge and angled my body to work my way up the concrete side edge of the window frame with my feet. That would take some of the weight off my hands. About eighteen feet or so and I would be able to get to the vents. Up close I noticed that Jesus' mouth had no teeth. The ground cable was cutting into my hands, but I made it high enough to catch my foot in the first vent and rested a second. I wiped some blood from my hand on my pants. All the dried bat droppings made the louvers dusty and slick. It was daylight, so I figured I wouldn't bother the bats. Wouldn't want them dropping out like fallen angels as they do every evening at dusk.

I could slide my hands up into the louvers and use them for climbing. It was much easier than I thought. I wondered why the teenagers hadn't figured this out for fun. A pigeon fluttered off the tower, its wings flappy and squeaky. I paused a minute to flex my fingers, one hand at a time. There was another set of windows above me. Small with geometric designs. God's calculus of perfection I assumed. At least they did not take up the entire width of the tower.

I could climb up beside them. But my hands were getting the best of me. Cut and tired, I needed some help. I reached down to slip off one shoe and pull off my sock. Then the other. I used the socks as gloves. The shoes made quiet "thunks" as they landed in the flowers. Figured my feet could better stand the punishment. Grip the edges of the vents with my toes a bit. I was worried a minute I might slip and fall. But then, I was climbing the tower in order to jump.

The grip was better. My hands cushioned. I felt assured I could make the pinnacle. I now found that I had plenty of energy. I guess as they say, "You can't take it with you." It would be my final expenditure. I reached the fortress notch at last and pulled myself through. This disturbed a whole flock of pigeons who ignored the warning of the solo pigeon who took off earlier. They seemed surprised. Well, maybe they don't get many visitors. Besides the squirrel, of course. The crow, now in the top of the tallest oak, cawed a greeting. Although I reckon you could interpret the sound as a negation- "Nuh uh. Nuh uh."

I caught my breath and took a look around at Everton. What a different take on the town you can get from up here. Familiar buildings had unfamiliar rooftops. An old mop stood leaning against an access door. Rusty tar buckets stood filled with rainwater. Flocks of pigeons walked in fields of their own waste. Down below, cars and pedestrians negotiated and maneuvered. Whatever important business went on in these buildings was all shielded by flat metal or tar and gravel roofs. A few with sagging trusses and rotten shingles covering gables. The church roof below me was copper. Green with age. The cross at the far end of the roof was the same material. Two squirrels chased each other, thumping and scratching in circles on the slick metal. I pulled myself up on the parapet wall and sat in a half lotus position. Took the socks from my hands and rubbed my wounds for a minute. Massaged my bare feet and gave them a good dusting.

A lady down below walked a small fluffy white dog on a red leash through the church yard. A red collar circled its neck. The dog lifted a leg to mark a gravestone. The woman stopped and stood in a locked position looking off in the distance. The little dog walked around behind the granite slab sniffing intensely. Its mistress took a pack of cigarettes and a book of matches out of her purse. Her motions, so often practiced, were smooth and unthinking. Quite natural, instinctual, like the dog. A long plume of smoke rose up through the oak branches. She flicked the match stick off into the grass. The dog was squatting, taking a dump on some long forgotten grave. Maybe she was pretending not to notice. Or she came unprepared for the dirty deed. But the woman started walking, indifferent, not bothering to pick up after her dog. Not even looking to see what the dog was doing. Its slick shiny calling card instead of a vase of flowers marking the middle of the plot. All was quiet except for the jingle of the dog's tags on his collar as he walked with a springy motion. Then I heard a voice. Who would be up here talking? A familiar voice startling me, which at first I didn't recognize as my own. "Mam. Oh, Mam, excuse me! Up here! Up here! I'm afraid I need some help getting down..." My voice trailed off. The woman tilted her head back. And then further back, adjusting her glasses and squinting. Trying to figure out what she was seeing. She looked down for a moment. I could see her shoulders start to shrug and shake. She looked up in pure wonder, and started laughing. Cigarette smoke illustrating each sound. A loud boisterous laugh. As though she were in the audience at some comedy. The squirrels began to chatter. The crow cawed repeatedly. The chorus continued as though it would never stop. Then I began to laugh.

perry neel

## The Ingenuity of Solitude

Father Brown placed a handwritten copy of his upcoming sermon on Dorothy's desk. "I'm off for a hospital visit" he announced while glancing at the mirror to adjust his stiff white collar. He slicked back his hair with the palm of his hand. "I won't be back, so I'll get it on Sunday," he said, giving a nod toward the notebook.

"Whew. I never thought he would leave," Dorothy mumbled to herself. She flipped the switch to turn on the typewriter, but stood up and pushed the sermon aside. "I haven't got this one trained right," she thought. Father Brown was used to big, powerful churches, where he was king. Now, near the end of his career, he was coasting with this smaller, easier parish. Still, he was accustomed to being served. Dorothy was tempted to tell him "There is no imperial priesthood at St. Peter's." The previous rector dialed his own phone calls. Typed his own sermons. In fact, you would have to go back three prior rectors to find a time when Dorothy took dictation or typed sermons. "His are such a bore, too," she said out loud. "I don't want my hands associated with them." Besides, she had enough to do with the bookkeeping and committee reports. She used to have all of Friday just to get the church bulletins right.

"I need a drink." She hoped for whisky but settled for the soda machine. The ancient floor boards creaked as she walked the hallway. Dorothy stopped to lock the front door of the Parish House and turned out the lights. It was 2:30. No one would be coming in on Friday afternoon. Except for somebody looking to raid the Rector's Discretionary Fund with some scam. "But the Rector's not here," she chuckled. The lock clicked. Dorothy had heard enough of the needy's sad tales in her thirty years at St. Peter's. Most of them were con-artists. She knew who the real cases were. But she could smell the liars and cheats. They would stink up the hall before they ever got to the office door.

The old church kitchen was cluttered with long forgotten Pyrex dishes and plastic tubs. Each pot-luck dinner contributed to the stock of unclaimed containers. The sink was filled with dirty dishes. "Thirty years and still nobody cleans up after themselves." She opened the refrigerator to see if there were any leftover soft drinks from the youth meeting. Empty. Lots of left-over food, though. "Those kids drink up every free soda in the house." So she reached in the pocket of her dress for some change and jingled out a handful to sort. Dorothy dropped a quarter, and then another, some assorted dimes and nickels until she tallied the total for a drink. She figured it would owe her a nickel in return. She waited for each coin to clink its way down before adding the next. The machine could be finicky and eat your money if you pushed the button too soon. Diet Coke. The can plummeted down the shoot and landed with a thud at the bottom. She reached for it with her left hand and waited for her change with the other. Nothing. She waited. Not a clink. Dorothy tapped her right foot. Then bopped the machine with the side of her fist. She checked her rings. She had just gotten her diamond reset after 43 years of marriage. Her husband was long gone, but diamonds are forever. Dorothy pounded the red machine right on the dented spot in the word "Coke." It had taken a beating over the years.

"Damn it." She looked instinctively over her shoulder toward the door. Just checking to see that she was alone so that no one heard her profanity. Though she did it often, she preferred that it not be known.

Dorothy's Scottish blood would not allow her to come short a nickel. "I want my change," she demanded and squirmed her index finger up the change slot. "It must be hung up in here, somewhere." She thought she could feel the edge of a coin so she twisted her finger in deeper to try and pry it loose. Nothing came out. Not even her finger.

Dorothy wrenched and turned but it wouldn't budge. She got down on her knees and tried to extract her finger with a downward pull using her free hand. Her knee knocked over the can she had placed on the floor. The Diet Coke rolled across the kitchen linoleum and settled under the stove. Starting to panic, Dorothy pulled hard and felt a sharp pain of metal digging in. She looked out the window and grimaced. A bright afternoon sky. She slumped to the floor to sit. Her finger was snagged. No one would be back until Sunday.

Thinking more effort might dislodge the finger, she spun around on her behind and put both feet on the machine. It wasn't graceful, but these weren't graceful times. She pushed with her feet and strained back. Nothing. She could feel her digit throbbing.

Swelling quickly, only to tighten the hold.

She called for help. Nothing. The Parish House was too far from the sidewalk and traffic on the street was too noisy. "Help!" Then she remembered reading somewhere that people are more likely to respond to the cry of "fire" than of "help." "Fire!" She waited. "Help!"

Tears swelled up in Dorothy's eyes. She knew she wouldn't die there. But sitting on the floor for two nights with her finger stuck up a Coke machine was too much. Then more bad news. "I'll get hungry!" She tested her reach with her free hand. She grasped the refrigerator handle. "Good," she sighed. She wouldn't starve. But what about the bathroom? The tears came in a torrent. To be found Sunday morning in her own squalor. Then, drawing on another part of her Scottish heritage, she knew she had to pull herself together. Courage. Dorothy checked her watch and calculated. Forty two hours. Forty two hours shackled to a vending machine. She steeled herself, preparing to meet the duration of her captivity.

Dorothy slumped back against the wall perpendicular with the drink machine. She sat for a full hour, finger in the slot, head hanging down. Solitude. Reflecting on fate, she wondered whether an old woman could come to some epiphany. At best an experience of grace on this retreat in the hermitage of the church kitchen. What grand lesson must be the divine rationale for her plight? She felt like a nun in midnight anguished prayer. The red glow from the Coke sign hovered over her head as the twilight fell, the sunlight gracefully receding over the city. Dorothy slept the sleep of the innocent. She dreamed of her husband and Sunday drives of times past. The leaves rushing in a whirlwind behind the car. The gentle squeeze of his hand around hers. She awakened with a stiff neck, a really sore finger, and arm numb. "A hell of a note," she muttered. "Dreaming of Jack like that. Funny thing, in my sleep I forget about him running off with that young girl."

She climbed to her feet and staggered with stiffness. Her knees creaked and every move revealed something about old age. The finger was lodged tight. Her whole hand red and starting to swell. But in a practical frame, "I'm kinda hungry," Dorothy thought. Stretching out her free arm, she leveraged the refrigerator door, then picked through moldy cheese, stale bread, and rotting vegetables. Though not in a position to be choosy, nothing looked appetizing at all. She turned over an oozing tomato when the revelation struck. Without a moment's contemplation, Dorothy grabbed a stick of butter and bit off half of it. She rolled it around like a communion wafer in her mouth. It slowly began to soften and melt. She waited till oil dripped from the corners of her lips. She savored it and dropped to her knees. Turning her face up to the heavens she leaned forward and placed her lips next to her finger, pursing them against the slot, like a kiss on the bishop's ring. Gently she spewed the fatty liquid up into the changer, blowing the melted butter as hard as she could. The butter drenched her finger and dripped down her hand and off onto the floor. It dripped like candle wax on the altar. Carefully, Dorothy twisted and with a slight tug delivered the finger from its captivity.

Dorothy walked over to the sink, grabbed a coffee mug and filled it with cool water. She rinsed her mouth while running the faucet over her red and swollen finger. Then she wiped her face and hands with a paper towel. Reaching under the stove, she retrieved the warm Diet Coke. Dorothy turned out the light in the kitchen and walked down the hall to her office. She sat at the desk and popped open the can, careful not to use her sore, swollen finger. She thought how pleasant an ice cold can would feel right now. But it was room temperature. She wasn't the type to waste. She took a sip and placed the can beside Father Brown's sermon and started to type. Sunday's sermon title: "Waiting on God."

## Truth

It was still hot the first of September in Southside Virginia. It wasn't unusual at all to have a few ninety degree days before summer sputtered out of fuel. Moss usually enjoyed the heat till about mid-August. But this year, after the July simmer, it seemed like the pot burned dry. Besides, it didn't make sense that the boys down at Hampden-Sydney were preparing for the season opener next Saturday. "A boy once cooked his brains in that helmet. Played in near 100 degrees," he overheard old Comer once observe.

Comer wasn't there this year. He hadn't missed a Labor Day stew in forty seven years. As much as people became fixtures around Nottingham, they really didn't miss them much either. When you're gone, you're gone. No one had even mentioned him. Comer always came early to start the fire under the ancient black kettle. Said there wasn't much need for everyone to stand around waiting for the pot to boil. "Don't need to come till it's time to stir," he always explained. So mid-morning on Labor Day, for probably close to half a century, old Comer drove around the village in his battered, blue Dodge truck picking up quart jars from all the ladies while the pot heated up. Took them down to the churchyard and set them on the picnic table for the flies to inspect. He'd stoke the fire with a few extra logs and wait. By then it was time to stir and he expected others to do the pleasure while he sat on a stump for a good chew.

It was Comer who had re-introduced Moss to a good chew. "Red Man" to be exact. "Anybody who's a man knows a good chew," is all Comer had to say about the subject. Moss remembered his mother throwing a fit and making him wash his mouth out with peroxide when he was a teenager. He hid the fact that he chewed until the first summer he came home from Virginia Tech. He would sit out on the porch in the dark, after a long day helping on his uncle's farm, and chew. His mother came out one evening and Moss tried to hide the big wad of Red Man in his cheek. Kept his face turned to the shadows. His mother went on for what must have been twenty minutes about the women in the church choir. Moss thought he would throw up from not getting a chance to spit. Finally, his mother said "You must be good at chewing. I haven't seen you spit once since I came out here." Then she jerked him up by the sleeve and to the bathroom for a peroxide cleanse. Moss felt about eight instead of eighteen.

Moss tried to keep on chewing. He kept it hidden from his mother and pretty much everyone else for a while. It was considered redneck at Tech. Then it became cool. Then the Surgeon General's warning. Tech even banned cups from the library. Drinking was always forbidden, but clever undergrads like Moss figured the rule wouldn't apply to a cup used as a spittoon. Then the baseball coach banned chewing tobacco. So Moss gave in. Big wads of bubble gum and a lot of spitting on the infield dirt. At least to keep up appearances.

Now, having been an adult for some time, he reverted to chewing, thanks largely to Comer and his certain manly outlook. It was another year, and another Brunswick stew. And no more Comer. But a pouch of Red Man bulged in his hip pocket.

It was awfully hot standing near an open fire, but Moss relished his turn with the paddle. It was not particularly fun, even boring. But it was a rite for the men of Nottingham. Two hundred people or more turned out every year to eat Brunswick stew and hear a rousing patriotic speech which no one remembered an hour later. There were plenty of big events in the neighboring bigger towns on Memorial Day and the Fourth. But Nottingham found a niche for itself on Labor Day. People could do a little politicking, a lot of gossiping, and eat some fairly mediocre stew.

Moss reached in his back pocket for some Red Man. He held the paddle under his arm and wiped the sweat from his forehead with the back of the hand holding the pouch. Joe Smiley walked up wearing his usual straw hat with the little green window in the visor. His big grin showed off a fine set of teeth stained by many years of Red Man. "Need a break, Moss?" he asked. "No thanks, Joe. Just stopped to get a little chew. I'll stir a few more minutes."

"Nice crowd, wouldn't you say?" Everyone always said things like "Nice crowd" or "Look how them children have grown." Even though Moss had lived six years in Richmond after college before coming back to take over the insurance office when his dad died, nothing had changed much in Nottingham. "Pttt," Moss ejected a tobacco stem from his mouth over toward the elm tree. "Sure is a nice crowd," he added. "I've 'bout got my last pole beans, if you want some, come on by," Joe announced. "Sure," Moss replied in the best minimalist fashion, the way Nottingham men were known to talk. Moss and Joe both spat long streams of brown juice toward the elm.

"Hey Moss, how' you, hon," Ruby MacIntyre chimed as she strolled up in a bright floral house dress, fanning her breasts with a handkerchief. "Fine, Mam." "Joe, you heard about Effie Ann, haven't you?" Moss turned away because he knew Ruby and Joe were about to have a semi-private conversation about a cousin they shared whose life was a continuous litany of sorrows. Childhood illness, widow during the war, divorced, son in prison. The kind of person who seemed not just to live, but flourish off of catastrophe. Moss wondered why people worried about her. He heard Ruby say something about gallstones, as she and Joe rotated to the left of Moss toward the elm tree, seeking more privacy. The juices swelled up in Moss' cheek. Half intent on catching what Ruby was telling Joe, he turned the opposite way to use his good ear. And spit.

"Damn!"

"What was that, hon?" Ruby looked back over her shoulder at Moss. "Oh nothing," Moss muttered while wiping at his mouth with his forearm. He looked a bit flushed. And quickly turned around to survey the crowd in the churchyard. "You look all hot, sugar," Ruby added. She stepped away from Joe to get a closer look at Moss.

"Let me take over," Joe requested. "You do look overheated."

Moss wasn't overheated. The red face was embarrassment. He had spit in the stew.

Joe walked over and took the paddle from Moss and started to stir. Bewildered, Moss took his red bandana out of his pants pocket and wiped his neck and face. Looking around again, he was confident no one had seen it. He tried to explain to himself how it happened. He had been spitting over to his left until Ruby took Joe over to the elm to talk. He must have gotten disoriented and the sudden urge to purge himself of the juice happened so quickly. He spit right down in the kettle. "Oh, shit," he thought. "What will I do?" "Two hundred people here ready to eat." And, "Oh no, Benny Parson," the rotund, native son, Baptist preacher was walking up the church steps to the spot where he always welcomed the crowd and rendered the blessing.

Moss sat down by the elm. He felt weak when he saw the children lining up at the head of the table where Mrs. Jenkins was opening a big bag of plastic soup bowls. Her grandson stood beside her, twisting the hem of her dress with one hand and gnawing on a spoon with the other. Mrs. Relf, the school librarian picked up the ladle to fill the glass jars for take home.

Parson started to pray, "Almighty and everlasting God, giver of all good gifts..." Moss slumped down further, his mind in agony. "What can I do?" "...and thank you for this stew, prepared by blessed hands and seasoned by your grace..." "Seasoned by Red Man," Moss said half out loud. He jumped up and raced toward the kettle, half waving his arms to stop the proceedings. In his path Joe stood grinning, gently stirring the stew through the end of the prayer.

"I seen you do it, Moss," Joe said in a low voice and spit down next to Moss' feet. "You did?" Moss was ashamed but half relieved. "What should we do?" he pleaded in a low, secret tone. "Same thing I did twenty years ago. Keep stirring and serve it with a smile." "Yu-Yu- You did it, too?" Moss stammered. "Yep. But old Comer

perry neel

told me it was the secret recipe he had known for years."

# Redemption

"No Betty, I feel worthless. Emasculated. I don't know how to describe it, but I'm not sure I'll ever feel like a man again."

It was with those words, or something like them, that I poured out my pain to my therapist, Betty. I WAS worthless. Unemployed and trying to finish graduate school in anthropology. My wife left me, for a woman no less. If anything could cut the manhood out of a guy, it would be that. Short of going through the pubescent initiation of a New Guinea tribe, I felt like nothing could restore me. My childhood crying and running to my mother with every hurt, my teenage failure to make the high school baseball team, the acne that kept me from a real date until I reached college... all prolonged my venture into manhood. It was a pitiful adolescence. My old pal Jerry and I used to ride around the school parking lot on Saturday nights. We'd see heads bobbing up and down in backseats, and pick up a pair of panties or stockings dropped from an open window in the heat and fury. That was as close to manhood as we could get. It felt like not much had changed.

My victorious entry finally occurred with Margie. A blind date brought us together at the University of Richmond. She was the most beautiful sight I had ever seen. Her platinum hair, light blue eyes. Reminded me of the white Studebaker Hawk that I restored in high school. I always thought it would get me girls, but it was the sale of the Hawk that got me to UR, and ultimately, Margie. With the Hawk long gone, and Margie recently departed, I entered my thirties with two strikes and felt I was flailing away at a low and outside curveball.

I spent most evenings rolling around on the couch, alternating between TV, magazines, and the radio. It was on a Saturday night that I heard a steamy voice that roused my manhood again. It was a local jazz program from the public radio station. The voice belonged to Cecily Woods. A most beautiful voice. Sensual and deep, with a smoky rasp. Perfect for jazz. Her voice was music itself. Cecily was as mysterious to me as this newfound discovery of melancholy music. I had drifted from a lifelong appetite for rock & roll and found this somber stirring music better suited my current sensibilities. And Cecily sparked something in me that no sound alone had ever done. In the melancholy deep swell of jazz, it was a voice that joined with me in my solitude. I tuned in every Saturday.

My friend Rick worked part-time at the radio station to make a few extra bucks. He was trying to survive UR as well. He did the late night engineering and announced the station breaks. I called him one Saturday night as soon as I heard Cecily on the air. "I can see her right now from the control booth, right across the studio in one of the broadcast booths" he told me. "Why don't you come down and visit the station. I'll introduce you." That easy? I thought Rick was teasing me.

"No, I can't do that," I stalled.

"Come on, man," he pleaded. "We can sit around the station

and when there is a break, I'll introduce you. Then we can go get a beer when I get off." Rick knew my limitations. Throw me in, but pull me right back out.

I mustered the courage. "Yeah, it's been a while." Since Margie left I had not spent much time with Rick. Or anyone else. He was trying to pull me out of my hermitage. "I could use a beer," I said. I was trying to deflect my overly obvious interest in meeting Cecily. So out the door and into the Buick.

It had been about a year since I was last at the station. But I remembered its complicated layout. A concrete block building right at the base of the broadcast tower on the edge of town. I knew which door would be unlocked and went straight through to the engineer's fishbowl. Rick swung open the door and offered his big hand with a cup of coffee sloshing in it. "You take it, cream only, I recall?" Coffee, the staple diet of radio. We sat down to talk, the sound of jazz, low and silky coming through the speakers. I sank deep into the old secondhand couch. But Rick immediately lifted his hand like some Indian guide pointing to the great valley. I followed his finger across the lobby and through the plate glass window. I saw a woman, dark and shadowy, spinning around in a swivel chair, adjusting knobs and tilting the microphone. A big set of headphones squeezing her face. Then over the station's intercom, the voice. It rose gently then faded down and blended into the rising swell of another tune.

She was not as I had pictured. Is it ever the case? Well, I really couldn't decide what she might look like. Her curly dark hair had a pleasant earthiness. Her eyebrows thick, her eyes dark and deep.

She was slender and tall.  I could tell that even though she was seated.  Her lips were full and although I never really liked for people to smoke, the cigarette in her mouth reminded me of Bacall. If only I knew how to whistle.  It all fit together.  She wasn't the most beautiful woman I had ever seen, that was still Margie.  But the mystery of it all sure made Cecily the sexiest.

Before I could utter a syllable to Rick, he was out the door, waving his arms frantically as one would to get a deaf person to avoid some tragedy.  Cecily looked up, smiled and dropped her cigarette into an ashtray.  The way she pulled off the headset was as erotic to me as Kathleen Turner taking off her dress in "Body Heat." I shuddered a bit, stunned.  Rick was motioning me out into the lobby.

"Cecily, I want you to meet my old buddy, Ben.  Ben, Cecily Woods."  She stuck out her hand and I didn't know what to do. Luckily, reflexes took over.  Her grip was firm.  I felt it pull on my entire body like the undertow at Virginia Beach.

We talked a couple of minutes in the lobby while the record played.  But I can't remember about what.  Suddenly, she grabbed my hand and whirled me around, pulling me behind her.  Said something about "...damned record's over..."  Cecily dragged me into the booth, threw me in a chair and slammed the door.  Tilted the mic and gently raised the slide button on the control panel.  "This is the Paul Winter Consort..." and with a flick of her left hand the turntable rolled.

We talked during the records for the next hour and a half.  Rick sat across the way doing his job.  I heard about her divorce, her child, her real job as a computer analyst for the commonwealth, the radio show which she did as a hobby. The conversation so matter of fact. My enchantment one of those facts. I hung on every word. When the show was over we stayed in the studio. She solicited my opinion about several jazz samples, though I really knew nothing at all about jazz. She was considering what to play next week. At about 1:00 in the morning I found the courage to ask her if she wanted to go somewhere for a drink. She declined, and I was disappointed, saying that everything would be closed by the time we got there anyway. But then she offered for me to follow her in my car over to her house for a drink. Before I knew it I was weaving my way in my old white Buick through the Richmond night over to Cecily's house off Laburnum Road. We left poor Rick alone, but I am sure he was pleased.

Cecily uncorked a bottle of wine in her kitchen. I leaned against the counter while she told me her daughter was away visiting her father. "I want you to hear this," she said, pulling me by the arm again. Into the living room. I sat on the sofa and Cecily sat in a big round rattan chair across the coffee table from me. She played a record and the placid sound quickly merged with the placid intoxication from the wine. During my depression I had not done much drinking. I must have been extra vulnerable to alcohol. Our conversation was nothing to get worked up about. I couldn't tell if she was even interested in me. Probably just someone to talk to. Still, being present with the woman whose voice seduced me every Saturday night was living a fantasy. But why was she spending time with me? Should could be with any guy in Richmond, why me?

The dark room was illuminated by only a small lamp and the glow from the stereo. I said little. Just listened to Cecily and the music, which were mostly one and the same. I was in the paradox, being so attracted to her, but not knowing and really not wanting her to be attracted by me. I wasn't sure I would know what to do if something happened. A tightrope of lust and fear, giving way to wine. I think I almost drifted to sleep somewhere around 4. Drowsiness trumping enchantment. As drunks often find, the body takes its instructions from something other than the mind, I suddenly rose to my feet and announced that I had better go. I had said the words before even having the thought. She acknowledged the hour and her appreciation for my coming over. "I'm glad we had this time, Ben."

Out on the porch I was hoping to do better than the old southern tradition of taking forever to leave. I wouldn't be able to handle an oozing departure. It was cold and I was concerned about driving across town this tired and drunk. Just wanted to say bye and hop in the car.

"Thanks again for coming...Let me kiss you goodnight." I expected a friendly peck on my cheek and a quick departure in the old Buick. What I got was an embrace that pulled me up tight against her body and a kiss that quickly brought sobriety. Reminded me of the time lightning struck the flagpole once when I was playing centerfield. I was in an electrified tingle, hairs standing on end. It must have gone on for ten minutes out there on the porch. My sweat contradicted the forty degree morning air. A redemption of my manhood was more than I could take. Could I live up to the passion and fire of this sultry advance? I knew her life experience far exceeded mine. The men she must have known made the varsity in high school. They were the ones bouncing their daddy's cars up and down in the backseat with some cheerleader. I wanted to run. I didn't want to be tested. Not yet.

"I wish we could make love," she whispered. Her lips brushed my ear, like a strike-anywhere matchstick. I knew I would only disappoint her and further dig myself into a hole. I wasn't ready for this. What could I do? But before I could even make up some ridiculous excuse like an old war wound, she added, "But we shouldn't." Words of absolution if I ever heard any. A gentle, friendly push from Cecily and I was down the steps and in the Buick.

I told Betty at my session that Tuesday that I had been reborn. Gave her the whole story, every little detail I could remember. The jazz show. Her voice. The radio station. The conversation. The drunkenness. Music. Euphoria. Fear. The kiss. What she whispered... "Knowing that she wanted to, but I didn't have to, that was just enough," I said. I had gotten out of there, dignity intact. Realized I could be both in and out of the arms of a woman at the same time. Betty and I were both near tears laughing so hard. I was starting to feel like a man again. One small step at a time.

perry neel

# Promise

"Well, are you in- or ain't ya" old Borden growled across the formica topped table. Jake pressed his elbows down hard and scrolled his eyeballs up and down from the aged Borden to his stained, dog-eared cards. Up and down he looked, until he scanned right and left. Uncles Fred and Bert and some distant cousin of his wife whose name he could not remember sat to his flanks. Ever the outlaw, Jake now keenly felt the pressure to live up to his in-laws. This summer ritual of the menfolk gathered on the screened porch playing poker had its manly appeal. Yet also the unpleasant expectations of family. That is, his wife's family.

Jake flipped the edges of the cards. In college days he would have comfortably bluffed his way through the game. He never quite developed the skills of poker playing, but being with the guys was the important part. Here, he didn't feel like one of the guys. He did not share their politics or their religion. Their values were different. But they shared that all-encompassing, like it or not, bond - family. Which to the Bordens, overrode all differences. Even a well-educated yankee, young Democrat like Jake found acceptance in that genial, gentlemanly, southern fashion.

Jake never understood the family thing. His life had been one of paying your respects to the family, but beyond that, if you wanted to enjoy your life, you stayed away from them. The Bordens on the other hand, took every occasion to get together. From near and far, they flocked to this small (dilapidated, considering the money they all had) cabin overlooking the James River. A shack that had grown weary of too many years and too many people. But they loved it. Not Jake. He felt claustrophobic at these family holidays. The screened porch reached half way around the house, but they always left on the winter plastic covering. There was no fresh air. The place sweltered in the Tidewater summers of Virginia. Too cheap to air condition the place.

"Are you in, Jake?" Bert inquired. Bert was the more relaxed of the Borden breed. He seemed a bit more open minded than the rest. "Dr. Pepper you know. 10, 2, and 4, all wild," Fred's reminder condescended.

"In, I guess," Jake waffled. His three 3s were hardly a source of confidence. Old Borden spread out his hand. Four Kings. With a gleeful swipe of his calloused and veined hand, he cleared the chips across the table up against his belly. Then stacked them into triple towers of red, blue, and white. "Sorry, son." Jake imagined it was the same tone of voice Borden used when he took that part-time funeral assistant job after his retirement. "Sorry, mam, I know we'll all miss him" Jake imagined him saying.

"I'm out of money," Jake apologized as he stood up from the table. He was glad to be out. His back and seat stuck to the vinyl chair.

"Hang on partner." Fred grabbed Jake's hand and pulled him back down to his chair. "Bert, get this young man another beer. Borden, lend yo son-in-law some money so he can stay in this game."

"Really, it's getting late. Sarah and I have to get the girls back to Richmond early tomorrow."

"Come on Jake, just another couple of hands," Borden insisted. He poured himself another splash of bourbon. Then another for both of his brothers. The cousin shook his head, "No." Jake reluctantly agreed. He knew it would be like last summer when he lost more than he could afford. He took another loan from his father-in-law and the next day Sarah was none too pleased. But then, Borden managed to never let Jake repay him. And he always resented having to owe.

"What will it be, Jake?" Fred asked. Jake looked up at the big clock style thermometer on the wall. It read 82, even at this hour long after sundown. Jake looked at the cards. His hand had been dealt.

He put down three. "Hit me three times." Jake was embarrassed that he sounded like Borden. A good old boy playing cards. The thought that the old man was rubbing off on him was alarming. He rubbed at the sweat on his can of Pabst.

"Are you in?"

"Sure," Jake replied. Without looking at his cards, he slid the whole pile of chips that Borden had given him to the center of the table. A pile of rubble on top of the grazed red formica. He figured the quickest way out was to blow his hand. Which he did.

As he started to rise from the chair, in mid-sentence of repeating something about getting back to Richmond, old Borden stood and reached across the table with both hands pushing Jake down by the shoulders, forcing him to sit. "You ain't goin' nowhere," he growled. Jake just now caught on to the effect the bourbon was having on the old man. It was late and Borden had kept a glass in his hand all afternoon and evening. Jake had never seen him drunk, and surely never unpleasant. But an unpleasant force of authority emanated from the old man.

"Every year you lose my money at this poker game," he snarled. "I should've kept tab, but I didn't."

"Here, I'll pay you back right now," Jake countered while reaching to see if his checkbook was in the back pocket of his khakis.

"No, no, no. I don't want your money. It's not the money," the old man lectured. "It's something else. Respect, something like that, I don't know." Borden fumbled to bring thoughts to words. A quick glance around the table showed that Jake was not alone in his surprise. "Win, lose, I don't care. It's not the money. I got plenty of money. It's family. I'm here, you're here. We're here. It's family. None of us cares who wins." The old man wheeled his head around to meet each individual eye to eye. "But you're not really here. As soon as you arrive you're gettin' ready to leave. You play this game, but you lose. You don't play smart, not because you are dumb. But because you think you are smarter than any of us." Borden's tired blue eyes stared right into Jake's.

Jake's ears were hot. He had never heard old Borden go off like this. Truth was, he was right. Jake was more embarrassed by being exposed. Then, maybe everyone already knew it. Sweat rolled down his sides and from his armpits dripping off his elbows. Little puddles formed on the broken tile floor. He sat silent for a moment, aware of the heat he would take from Sarah if he got in an argument with her father.

The old man leaned back in his chair and sipped some bourbon. "I just want you here with us," he mellowed. He even winked. Jake wondered how much was Borden and how much was Virginia Gentleman talking.

"OK," was all Jake could think to say. "OK!" he was emboldened. "I'll play you for real, if that is what you want."

"That's more like it, now we got us a game," Borden beamed.

"What are the stakes?" Jake asked. Deciding to get with the festivities he thought quickly for something high stakes. "How about my Karmann?" Jake figured the old man would be impressed by the offer of his old restored Karmann Ghia. His pride and joy. Not the kind of car Borden would ever like, but because he knew its value to Jake.

"The cabin," Borden countered. Jake figured the old man was convinced of his seriousness.

"The cabin. OK." He knew they would play it out, just for pride. And the wagers would be forgotten.

Bert, Fred, and the cousin sat out. They wanted to see the duel. They watched, both amused and intense. Borden shuffled, Jake cut, and the old man dealt. Straight up draw poker. The cards lay on the table until all were laid straight. Old Borden slid one card under the next until he had scooped up all five.

Jake flipped the cards over in his hand. A Queen of Diamonds, a 5 of Spades, an Ace of Diamonds, a Jack of Hearts. And a 9 of

Clubs.

Borden sat motionless, without expression. A practiced "poker face." Jake put down the five and the nine and called for two cards. His father-in-law also exchanged two. They sat in blankness for the better part of a minute. Fred coughed. The cousin scratched his head.

"OK, son," the old man nodded. Jake laid down the Ace, the Queen, the Jack, a two, and another two. A pair of twos. "Not much here," and Jake felt his hand fish down his pocket for the car key to turn over.

Old Borden paused, then tossed his cards face down, his entire hand on the discard pile.

Jake had forgotten that day in the recesses of his mind. His divorce two years later and his subsequent move to Charlottesville had crowded his mind with too many instances to leave any room for that poker game. In fact, it was hard to recount any of the details to the lawyer from Norfolk who had called Jake to inform him about Borden's will. Sarah called him three weeks ago to say her father had died. He felt sad for her. But now he finds that he has a trip to Norfolk to make. A long drive to claim the deed to the river cabin. A place he never liked was now his. If anything, old Borden was a man of his word. A promise was a promise. Nothing could change that. "Now, if only the old Karmann can make it down the highway for a three hour drive."

**No Place to Call Home**

I can't tell you which was worse. The smell of the diesel or the sour, greasy odor from the short order grill. Such are bus stations. Both probably contributed to my nausea. The line to my bus was long. Who rides buses these days? Well, I guess I'm finding out. When I finally board I am desperate to locate a suitable seatmate. Not the large woman with the 18 piece bucket of chicken. Nor the swarthy little man smelling of olive oil and whiskey. "Fort Worth," the driver read aloud from my ticket as though proving she were literate. I know where I am going. And it will be a long, long ride leaving Montgomery tonight. I'll have to transfer in Birmingham. Then on to Texas.

It's crowded. And hot. Generally two of my least favorite features of life. There will be no empty seat beside me tonight. But I spy a rather innocuous looking middle-aged man sleeping by the window. Sorta balled up like a roly poly in a blue checked shell. I quickly, and quietly as I can, slip off my backpack and stuff it in the overhead. I hold my other bag in my lap and fish around to find the book I've been reading. I watch where I put my big feet down in the darkness of the floor. I don't want to step on his. At least the air conditioning is kicking in. Much nicer than the steamy, central Alabama night.

I can't wait to get on the way. Two years of travel, under the guise of research, and a complete liquidation of all my assets. I am now too familiar with riding buses. I'm eager to get back to teaching. I never thought I would hear myself say that. The end of a marriage. Disillusioned by students. Disgusted with administration. I was rootless and restless at the time. Took my leave and the school gave me another year. Now, I'm weary of travel, of thinking. I look forward to a place to call home. The ideas I had about various subcultures in southern cities no longer reel in my head. It's about getting back to work. Getting back on track to a normal life. And first of all, finding a place to live.

The vacuum powered door smacks shut and we lurch out into the night. The driver turns off the interior lights and I reach for my personal lamp above my head, twist it on, and guide it to my book. I'm still not sure why a Sunday night bus from Montgomery to Birmingham would be full. Maybe they just run them once a day. I don't know. It is not long till we glide up the interstate ramp and the lady driver locks in at 70. The book is an anthology called "Peaceable Kingdoms." A bunch of utopian writings. I'm thinking at least I should get into my mind some sense of what people expect from society. At least, how culture could supposedly be at its best, maybe. Plato's optimally functioning "Republic." Johnson's "Great Society." Society? Great? Who knows? But is it perfectible? It still puzzles me why anyone, historically speaking, ever wanted more than security and the necessities. Locke, Hobbes, Smith, they were on the right track. Whoever thought that society can be perfectible? Only some elites and visionaries who long to make the kingdom of God on earth. And then get to brag about it! My research with poor people shows they never have such thoughts.

They know the world by its very nature is a rotten place. "Nasty, brutish, and short." Survival's the name of the game. Hah. Here I am, not even middle-aged and I have grown skeptical of visionaries.

The man next to me twists to a more comfortable position. I'm glad he's asleep. Not in the mood to strike up the obligatory conversation with my seatmate. Why do people need to talk to strangers? Being away for two years, I realized that I don't really want to talk much with the people I know. Although now I find myself thinking about the usual subject of talk among the anonymous, the weather. After all the heat and humidity, I'm catching a chill thanks to the bus AC. I see a bank sign thermometer over beyond the oncoming lanes. It reads 79 degrees and its 9:28 p.m.

I think I'll try to rest my eyes instead of reading. I fold the book on my chest. Flutter my eyes to clear them. Then I slide them shut. After months in Atlanta, Nashville, Memphis, Birmingham, Mobile, Biloxi, Montgomery, maybe I'm finally tired. Libraries, courthouses, churches, parks, front stoops.... all a blur to me now. Rental cars, cab rides, trains, buses. I guess you could say I'm travel weary. Especially tired of all the intellectuals and academics who describe and solve all society's woes and sleep comfortably in the suburbs at night. At least I got a firsthand look at how real people live. What their concerns are. I start to doze and immediately dream of East Lake Park in Birmingham. Little black children play at the edge of the water. Stirring up minnows and tadpoles with sticks. Splashing down hard on the water with a kickball. All the while, steel mills create an urban aurora borealis in the early evening sky.

I awaken briefly by the braking of the bus. We exit the interstate to some unknown small town. I did not see a sign, but it was not necessary. They are all the same no matter what the name. Little ghost towns with tentacle strips of fast food joints, car washes, car lots, and if the town is lucky, a bar. Bored teenagers cruising the streets in an endless ritual of looking for something without getting anywhere. A sheriff's car stood dark and silent in a bank parking lot. The bus pulled up to the curb. There was no station. No identifying sign for a bus stop that I could find. A couple get off, but I don't see anyone there to greet them. I close my eyes.

Next thing I know we are rolling off the interstate again, into downtown Birmingham. Surely I didn't sleep the whole way, but the evidence shows otherwise. I grab my bags and join the queue trudging off the Greyhound. Once in the station I search for a men's room. An easy feat in this squalid terminal. Just follow my nose. I'm standing at the urinal when I hear the call for Dallas-Fort Worth. Seems my trip home is almost too efficient. I zip and run.

The next bus is crowded, too. Again I settle for an aisle seat, repeating the same motions with my backpack and carry bag. The man at the window appears to be sleeping. Wait. He looks like the same one from the other bus. Blue checked shirt. Khaki pants. Uncombed dark hair. He lifts his head and turns an eye toward me. I was talking before I even thought about it. "Weren't you on the bus from Montgomery?" He nodded. Well, he must have walked straight onto this one. Or he possesses some magical transfer power.

Now that I initiated it, I feel the need to carry on a bit. Plus, I am a bit puzzled that he is already here and apparently sleeping again so quickly. After a few words, I ask the obvious question about his destination. "No place in particular." At first I take this to mean "None of your business." But my error is clear. It sounded about the same as someone saying "Chicago" or "Miami." In fact, he asks me the same. "Fort Worth," I tell him. He's friendly enough, I guess. Actually seems rather good natured for a bus passenger late Sunday evening. So maybe it will be a good way to pass some time with conversation. I normally dislike talking about myself, especially what I do, but he asks and I give him the lowdown. Teaching, my research travels, heading back home. I let it roll for a while, but I want to get back to him. Where is he going? Who rides to "No place in particular?"

After a few minutes, I feel like we have some trust. Some rapport. "So come on, where are you headed?" I take a second stab at it. "No place, really," his words downright chipper. I pause, then offer my name, figuring if I make it personal, maybe I can get somewhere. The researcher in me is turning detective. "I'm Joe McClendon." "Oh, Tom. Tom Moore." We shake hands. Now we are getting somewhere, I think. "Well, Tom, what is the destination on your ticket?" I really am playing cop now, as I wave my ticket, clearly marked "Fort Worth." His reply only frustrates my investigation. "Unlimited Pass." He draws it out of his shirt pocket to provide evidence.

For some reason his reply hits a raw nerve of curiosity. Like the little rivulets of water on the window from the drizzling rain out on the highway, his answer crept into the places with unaccountable shapes in my mind. Now I just have to know. So I take a different approach. I think I am really good at this. "Where are you from?"

"Nowhere."

My curiosity only intensifies, so immediately I do what frustrated debaters do. I take him literally. "You mean you come from no place and you are going no place?" I point my finger at a spot A in the air, then move it point B. Surely now I will be able to unravel the nuances. This man is hiding something. I want to know what it is. All those mindless detective novels I used to read for relaxation must have influenced me more than I know. I want clues. What crime? What murder? What is he running from? Notice the things I assume about human nature. All bad. And the one thing that I don't. That he can be a man from no place going no place in particular.

"Yes," Tom Moore replies. "It doesn't get any better." I didn't feel he was trying to cut me off. He sounds perfectly natural. Sincere.

So I try a different tactic. "How long, Tom?" Using his name might help me.

"Oh, I reckon about four years."

Four years? "Really?" It's the only possible reply.

"Yep. Think so." The truncated responses aren't diversionary. They come across well enough to convince a jury. It strikes me as odd that I am in a detective novel mode and not what I was academically trained for. Maybe our leisure choices more accurately reflect who we are?

"How did you come to do this?" I ask. "You just made a decision one day to drop what you are doing and ride around the country on buses."

"Pretty much."

I'm stunned. Who would choose this? Why? "What did you used to do?" I inquire.

"I was an attorney. I worked for the legislature in Maryland. Helped to draft the laws the politicians passed. Laws that might meet constitutional and legal standards. I hope that is not too complicated."

"Oh, no. I understand. I am a professor, you know."

"Well good... Do you mind if I try to sleep now? I think I'll get off in Louisiana and see what leaves outa there." He turns his head to the window and does the roly poly ball again. He looks well practiced at this mode of sleep. He doesn't wait for my answer.

I am surprised he cut it short. But he's not putting me off, I don't feel like. But I'd like to know why. And about family. Home. Where he grew up. Wouldn't anyone have a hundred questions for a man like Tom Moore? He gave up a good life, it would seem to me. And now rides buses to "no place in particular." This man had a real career. Doing what I would call important work. Still, I don't detect one bit of insanity. He is not, for what I can tell, a broken man. So, I sit quiet and still, pondering Tom Moore. Then I finally drift off to my own slumber.

I awake in darkness. Unaware of the passage of any time again. Tom Moore is gone. His seat vacant. I am not sure how he climbed over me. How he got his stuff. But he is gone. I slide over to stare out into the night. Nothing. Nothing at all. Then slowly, lights, signs of life. Houses. Businesses. Churches. The bus slides off on the shoulder to the right. It is one of those gas station rural stops. I have no idea where. I hear the vacuum gasp of the door. Someone enters and takes a seat up near the driver. Without thinking I pop up. Reach in the overhead and start up the aisle. The driver closes the door and releases the brake. "Wait." I shout louder "Wait!" A few heads stir. There is the rumbling of people changing positions. A muffled snore. I make my passage between the seats trying not to run into any hanging arms and heads with my bags. "You want off?" the driver asks. "Yes," I say. "This is not a rest stop, sir," she explains. "I know. I'm getting off here." "Well, OK, then." She pops open the door.

I step off into gravel, the door slaps shut and the bus glides behind me back onto the pavement. I have no idea where I am. The town is not yet stirring to life. If there is any life. The front of the gas station is lit up with a "Shell" sign and the glow from a couple of soft drink machines. The bay doors to the mechanic's garage are down. I have my backpack over one shoulder and the carry bag over the other. An unlikely pilgrim I must appear. I step onto blacktop where it is paved around the pumps. It runs up to the building. The sign says "Open 6 a.m. to 9 p.m. Every Day." I look for some indication as to where I am. I think it must be Texas. That's too far. Maybe still in Louisiana. Posters about church picnics, the Ruritan club, and a tractor pull fill the windows. No clues, though. Where am I? Then, above the door, on the frame separating the entrance and an old timey transom, I see something stenciled in black letters. It is hard to read because a bird's nest is dangling bits of stick and brown grass down over the words. I reach up and brush some of it away, trying not to disturb any occupants of the nest, if there are any. It reads, "Welcome to Utopia."

perry neel

## Grace

Grace Humphreys hitched up her violet stretch pants after placing the stack of documents on top of the copier. With her pudgy thumb she pried open the front cover of the machine and generously supplied the black powder to the reservoir. A broad sweep of her hand removed the scattered dust from the white plastic. She glanced curiously at the black dust now smeared along the creased lines of her palm. She looked for the "love line," the "marriage line," and the all-important "life line." She wasn't expecting a whole lot of good news. Trouble, she had come to accept. Jud, she imagined, was back home at the trailer sleeping off the refreshments from last night's poker game at Ned Latski's. She could tolerate that. Jud had given her eleven good years of marriage, give or take a weekend disappearance in 1983 and his penchant for Milwaukee's Best. He had somehow managed to work his way up from stocking tires and fixing flats at Burnley's Tire, to now where old Burnley himself says Jud is "The best retread man on the East Coast." Well, at least in Hexton, Virginia, she thought. She had come to take marriage, and her man Jud, the way they were. It was just how life turned out.

Grace slammed the cover shut and hit the "power" switch. She liked her job at Crossner's Insurance Agency. A little typing and filing and answering the phone beat the hell out of soft serve cones at the Dairy Doodle. Not many job options around here. She had worked at the dairy bar for four years after having her four children.

She would have settled for one kid, even none after that one arrived. But Jud had to have a son, as men are prone to want around here, just to keep the Humphreys name alive. It arrived three births later. Grace waddled her 236 pound form down the narrow hall from the filing room to the employee kitchen. The last few drops of coffee sizzled on the burner as the drip continued while she poured herself some "eye opener" into her favorite "Garfield" mug. She tended to picture herself as a sort of woman version of the cartoon cat. She fancied some rotund resemblance. Or maybe it was her blond hair dyed red that made it turn orange. Like "Roseanne" on the television, she thought herself cute and clever and enough to warrant more of her, even if it was more flesh. Grace poured the black Folger's and drifted back to the filing room.

The warm up light was green now, so Grace picked up the first sheet to copy. She slurped from the Garfield mug while the copies zipped through the machine. Suddenly the copier screeched to a halt. The red light blinked silently. "Aw, shit." She covered her mouth with her hand. She knew Mr. Crossner didn't like cursing in the office, remembering the dart of his eyes her first day in the office when she pinched her finger with a staple remover and said a few of her worst words. He was too much a gentleman to say anything. But she could read his eyes. He was a religious man, but then again, she was religious, too. He was a straight laced Presbyterian, while Grace went to the Holy John the Baptist Tabernacle down the road in Glenfield. She tried to serve the Lord as best she could. She knew the struggles of faith, having wrestled an angel a time or two in her life. Mr. Crossner, well, he was just one of those folks who was

94

born better than everyone else. He was nice and all, but she wondered if he really knew Jesus. The members at the Tabernacle, now they knew Jesus. Some even spoke in unknown tongues and wallowed on the floor like fish on the pier.

Grace piled the documents up on the shelf and opened up the copier again. A sheet of paper had caught in the carriage. She ripped it out in little pieces, wadded it up and plunked it into the waste can. She had to wait for the machine to warm up again and twirled some of her long stringy reddish blond hair over her right shoulder. Her arm wedged up under her huge breast which was secured under a bright orange and green print blouse. Her light brown eyes remained fixed on the light as kept blinking red. Soon as it switched to green she turned to pick up the papers and start the task all over again. Then she heard the "whirr" of the copier as it turned on. All by itself. "Strange," she thought and set the papers back down. "Must of bumped the button with my hip," she thought. After all, it was tight quarters and she pretty much filled any extra space. She reached with her right hand to pick up the sheet as it rolled out of the copier. Just as she started to float it into the trash, her fingers pinched the paper. "Sweet Jesus," she shouted. Though she was not in church. Her hand began to tremble and her arm shook as she held up to the window light a picture of her Lord and Savior, Jesus Christ.

Grace twisted her head back and forth in disbelief. This must be some kind of joke or something. A picture of the Lord coming out of a Xerox machine. She opened it up again to see the copy paper bin. She looked to see what was in the chute where the originals go.

Nothing there. Someone must have slipped it into the copy paper. She looked at the picture again. It was not quite like the ones in her family Bible. Nor was it like the one on the wall at the Holy John the Baptist Tabernacle. The one where Jesus is standing, knocking at a door. But there he was, the face of her savior, not smiling, not doing anything. Just staring up at Grace from a flat sheet of paper. She let it go and it fluttered like a sail and eased into the trash can. "Oddball sense of humor around here," she said quietly. Still wondering who would possibly play such a prank.

When she reached to put in a document the machine fired up again all by itself. "What's going on here?" It was loud enough to carry down the hall. "What you say, Gracie?" Lenora asked in her fine southern accent from the office down the corridor. "Oh, nothing," Grace shouted back. She had not intended to be heard. As the copy inched out of the machine, Grace could see the same top of the head, the long wavy hair, the Jewish nose, the creases around the lips, and the bearded chin. "Something is going on around here."

Quickly she fanned through the copy paper. Nothing there but plain white. She tore open the machine. Nothing in the carriage. Or on the drum. "God," she prayed. "I hope this is a joke. I'm getting the creeps." She kept it to a whisper so Lenora wouldn't come back there. Grace took a big gulp of coffee and shook out the cobwebs in her head.

She did not want to show Lenora. They weren't friends. Just co-workers. Lenora only worked to have something to do. She was a widow with money and fine clothes and no kids. She tolerated Grace. And Mr. Crossner was too serious a man and she was afraid he would think Grace was playing some sick sacrilegious joke. "Tommy," she suddenly blurt out. She figured it now. He was a sort to play practical jokes, the kind who would fart around, even if it involved using the Lord in vain. Tommy Wilkie was an agent working for Crossner. He grew up in Hexton. The age of Grace's little brother. They played football together for the Hexton High Diesels. Tommy once drove the school mascot, a diesel tractor, in the homecoming parade with a brassiere cupped over the headlights. A real jokester.

Grace waddled down the hall to the office. "Lenora, has Tommy been in this morning?" She knew she was about to resolve the mystery. "Why, no, Gracie. He's out of town at an underwriter's meeting."

"You didn't see him in the supply room yesterday afternoon by any chance?" Maybe he did it a day ahead to heighten the mystery? "No, he left yesterday morning. Why do you want to know?" "Oh, nothing," Grace trailed off. She didn't want to betray her private worry. Off she went back down the hall, rubbing her triple chin with her mitt shaped hand. "If Tommy didn't do it, then who?"

Once in the tiny room filled with shelves, filing cabinets, the copier, and now Grace, she bent down to pick up the two pictures of Jesus from the trash. They were identical copies. So she thought. But then one had a slight turn of the head to the right. She couldn't figure it out. She tried not to. Instead she had to rely on the simple faith she was taught at the Tabernacle. "Some things you can't explain. Just trust in the Lord." She knew that. But still, she kept thinking this had to be a trick.

Grace put in the claim form for Mr. Ricks, an old farmer on Highway 14 who ran his '74 Pontiac Catalina into a tree trying to avoid Mrs. Wiggen's cow, which had gotten through the fence. One thing Grace liked about her job was the gossip around Hexton. People were saying it sounded too much like the time Mr. Ricks ran into a ditch trying to miss a bear. Rumor had it there was a plastic milk jug in the back seat both times. And it wasn't spring water in it, either. The thought of the old man's escapades diverted Grace briefly from her serious crisis of faith.

She hit the "copy" button with her blunt index finger. The light flashed, the machine turned, and Grace reached for a paper clip with one hand and extended the other to grasp the product emerging from the copier. She clipped the original on top and as she laid the papers down on the little table the bottom sheet slid to one side revealing a bearded cheek bone, an ear, and a shoulder covered with hair. "Gracious Lord and Savior," she exhaled and clutched her heart and slumped. A box full of ballpoint pens rolled off onto the floor in a staccato clack, clack, clack. A neat stack of staple boxes tumbled down littering millions of little silver brackets across the floor. Grace gathered herself quickly as she heard Lenora click down the hall in her high heels calling "Grace, you alright?" with her feigned southern tone of concern.

"Just slipped on a ballpoint laying on the floor," Grace explained. She wadded up the Jesus pictures and shoved them to the bottom of the can. "Knocked all this stuff off the shelf, but I can get it."

"Grace, are you feeling ill? You look all pale, honey."

"Oh, clumsy me." Grace's tongue and lips were dry.

"Alright, hon," and Lenora clicked her way back to her office. No sooner than Lenora turned back, the copier came to life again and Jesus number 4 emerged.

"Still my fleeting heart, sweet Jesus," Grace whispered in prayer. She fanned her now pink face with her hand. Sweat beads were rolling down her forehead and between her breasts. "Tell me Lord, what are you trying to tell me?" She petitioned with her pudgy fingers now interlocked and inching upwards. "Is it something I done...or something I ain't done? Please tell me."

"I'm going down to Nick's Market," Lenora's voiced interrupted from down the hall. "You get the phone and see to customers?"

"Sure," Grace yelled back. Yet she was afraid to be left alone. She thought Crossner had stepped out earlier, and now there was no line of defense. Just between her and her Lord.

The Xerox flared up again, but Grace whirled around and fled down the hall. Flopping into her chair, she fumbled around her desk drawer looking for aspirin. She wondered if Lenora used tranquilizers. Maybe she could pilfer her desk. She needed something. Fast. But then her mind flooded with thoughts of Lenora's son's arrest, the psychiatrist, the pills. And the words of her pastor, "Pills are the devil's eggs. They always hatch demons."

Grace found instead her little black, pocket New Testament. Under some insurance applications in the top drawer. Like the Lord himself guided her hands. Maybe Jesus could show her what he is trying to tell her. Maybe those pictures were his way of making her listen to his Word. She flipped it open and her eyes were drawn to the red letters of Jesus' words. His response to the question about how often to forgive, "...till seven times? Jesus sayeth unto him, 'I say not unto thee, until seven times, but until seventy times seven.'"

"Forgive who?" she questioned out loud. Jud, for not being a good husband? Her mother, for not encouraging her to do better... for playing favorites with her siblings? Mr. Crossner for being so cheap? Pastor Dan, for looking after the attractive women in the congregation more than he ought to?

"Forgive who?"

Grace rose from her chair with great trepidation and crept down the hall to the copier. The machine was silent. She inched towards it, as one would approach a snake. She reached slowly to the tray and eased out the copies, afraid it might once again produce Jesus. Grace flipped through the pages. There were three more! "Seven." Now seven pictures of Jesus.

She stuck her hand to the bottom of the trash and fished out the others. She smoothed them on the table and rolled all seven like a church bulletin in your hand on your way out of church. She walked to her desk, eased open the top drawer and gently slipped them in. Like storing ancient scrolls in a museum vault. "Seventy times seven?"

All day Grace pondered the number. She periodically checked the Xerox, but no more. The excitement of the morning strangely turned to calm, like a summer storm when the clouds break up and the sun beams through the mist. She was pleasant to Lenora, Mr. Crossner, and all the customers. On the whole a good day, albeit a remarkable day. Grace revved up the El Camino to head home, pondering forgiveness. "Seventy times seven." She adjusted the rearview mirror, taking a quick glance at her plump, round race with the orange hair, and her toothy smile. Well, minus the one she needed to replace.

"I'm pretty blessed," she thought. "I'm not sure what you want to tell me, Lord, but I'm listening. Sorry you had to scare me like that. But I'm better now. Knowing you want to talk to me and all." She thought she would go home and tell Jud and kids that she just didn't feel like cooking tonight. Foot-longs at the Dairy Doodle would be a treat for them. And for herself.

perry neel

## A Twist

A twist of fate. I can't really tell if Uncle John's story qualifies for such dramatic treatment. It somehow strikes me that it is more sour milk. You get yogurt or buttermilk when it looks like all is lost. The cantankerous old bastard had forever been a pain in the family side. But if diamonds come from coal, then we should have expected the old jewel of a man John turned out to be.

When we were children, Uncle John always seemed amusing. His crusty clothes and tobacco stained teeth didn't become disgusting until we reached those disgusting teenage years. As soon as we started caring about how we looked, then we noticed with embarrassment how filthy and old John was. My parents and aunts all referred to him as "that dirty old man." A phrase they meant quite literally, not a description of perversity as it has come to be known. My uncles, they just shook their heads and looked down. No one had any idea what to do about him. He shaved about once a week and bathed even less. The whitish stubble on his hardened face made him look much older than he really was. Everything about him seemed old. He just looked it and acted it. A contrarian. Uncle John represented the generation of the great depression. His skinflint and dingy ways were dustbowl era. And he somehow managed to keep some of the dust with him. Never the type to talk about "the good ole days." He was a self-appointed embodiment of despair and dirt. A monument to an era his peers gladly left behind.

You could see the dirt in the creases and crevices of his face and neck. Under his thick yellow nails resided the depression, the dust bowl, prohibition, and World War II. The only analogy I can think of is the joints in the stones of the pyramids. Archaeologists should excavate the old man someday. When he dies, call a historian instead of a coroner.

John would irritate more people by doing nothing. He would sit all day on the porch of the house where he lived with his sister and brother-in-law. John was a widower and no one thought it proper for him to live alone. Anyway, he would just sit all day. Pretty much year round. Dirt must be good insulation. He didn't read. He didn't talk much. He just sat and watched. The children of the extended family would play in the yard after Sunday dinners. John just sat on the porch and watched. I didn't think he bothered anyone, but other members of the family grumbled about how he would come to dinner unbathed, that he never lifted a finger to prepare or cleanup after the meals. Nor contribute a nickel. It struck me as contradictory that they complained of having him near, then wanting him to pitch in. When I was about 6, I do remember his teasing me unmercifully about how I "didn't eat enough to keep a bird alive." I hid in my aunt and uncle's room and cried. That was the only time I remember really not liking him. Otherwise, I just didn't see much to care about. At times he annoyed the family with some narrow-minded proclamations about politics or social matters. George Wallace was not extreme enough for him. Washington is going to give everything to the niggers. And what this country needs is FDR. Boys are going to turn into girls if they don't cut their hair. That kind of stuff. I didn't care what he said, as long as it was nothing to me. But the adults cared. And took offense.

Before he retired from the coal company, where he worked a job I never understood, I gathered that John spent his money on beer and women. Once, he did take me and my brother downtown to what, in retrospect, looked like an old fleabag hotel. There was a cafe on the first floor. Really, more of a beer joint. While we ate grilled cheese sandwiches and drank Grapicos, he talked to a couple of plump ladies with lots of rouge on their cheeks. They were sitting at the bar nursing beers. After a while, one of the ladies came over and gave me and my brother candy bars. We smiled and said "thank you" as our father had taught us. But we never felt Uncle John had any such expectations of us. Why would he care if we were polite or not? He never was. He always said and acted as he pleased. In fact, I remember that very day he parked his big old Pontiac in the "No Parking" zone. To him, parking a car meant wherever it stopped. I sometimes wondered if he could read, he paid so little attention to written words.

Mary and Ralph, the two he lived with, were always feuding with John over something. There was the time John insulted their neighbor, Mrs. Wells. They never said what it was about in front of us kids. But now I suspect it was for taking a leak out behind the tool shed in broad daylight. Mrs. Wells was always in her garden just through the wire fence. "That man has no manners whatsoever," Mary would say, shaking her head like someone dealing with nagging aches and pains. They don't go away. One has to learn to live with them. Just like your own brother.

Then there was the time my cousin got married. He was the first of my generation to get married, so it was a big deal for the family. Ted's parents will never forget how John showed up at the wedding in a dirty shirt, no necktie or jacket. And at the reception he said something to the bride implying the necessity of their nuptials. Remarkably, Ted's bride is the only one who, to this day, treats Uncle John with any respect. As he grew older and less inclined to keep himself up, she would even trim his finger and toe nails for him. Her in-laws still hold a grudge. As does Ted.

Rumor has it that John never trusted banks. So he hid his money in his mattress. No one ever accused him of being clever. One of my cousins used to slip in John's room after Sunday dinner and slide under the bed and remove a dollar bill from the bottom of the mattress. The rest of us were either too honest or too afraid of the whipping we would surely get from our folks. I couldn't understand the cousin's restraint. He never took more than one dollar at a time.

So, you get the impression. The dirty old man, almost universally disliked. I could go on and on. There is the postman he kicked one time. The dog across the street. Well, they accused him of poisoning the dog. The two young girls on bicycles who claimed he exposed himself while they were riding down the sidewalk in front of the house. The socks he stole from his brother-in-law's bureau drawer. You get the picture.

Then, the day I found him sitting placidly in the glider on the front porch. He seemed to be smiling. He just smiled, that's all. I knew something wasn't right. So I went in the house to check with my aunt and uncle. They weren't at home. Turned out they had gone out to the discount store. So I took a seat on the glider beside John. And we waited. He just sat. And smiled. And we waited.

That was three years ago. A stroke. Fortunately John was not too physically impaired from it. He has a slight limp and his left arm tends to just hang. He never spoke anymore. Not a word. But that also meant no complaints. No insults. His insurance covered a little in-home nursing help. That means for once in his life, John stays clean. On the whole, what we got was essentially a yard gnome. Or a concrete angel statue. Maybe a family portrait of some idealized ancestor. Or as I like to think, because in my own backyard, a smiley happy Buddha. Clean him up, he stays clean. Wherever you put him, he stays put. Whatever the circumstance, nothing changes. No bad weather days. The birds could perch on his head and shit. No matter. Uncle John is now stuck with perpetual serenity.

From now on, I'm tempted to call him "Smilin' John." After all, he deserves it. Whatever he had been, as crabby and filthy as it was, he is no more. We should all be happy for him. And for us. Sometimes things do turn out alright.

perry neel

## Mother's Day

The same taxi driver pulled up to the curb in front of Fairlawn Presbyterian Church. He tooted the horn, which seem inappropriate on Sunday, even if the service was over. Mrs. Keegan stood alone, clutching her handbag, wearing a cheery springtime dress of yellow and white flowers. A small, almost indistinguishable flower, pinned to her lapel. She put her hand over her eyes like a salute, the sun making her hair a silvery blue. At first she couldn't spot the yellow Chevy, even though it stood in the no parking zone at the end of the sidewalk not more than fifteen yards in front of her. The Rev. Morton kindly stepped from a conversation to grasp her elbow and point to the waiting cab. At 77, she walked crisply, head high, tugging at the wrists of her white gloves. The driver jumped out as though sprung by the tolling of the noon hour from the church tower. He opened the rear door and as Mrs. Keegan slipped onto the seat, he reached to the front seat to retrieve a box of Hardee's chicken and handed it to her. "Your son said to pick this up and give it to you. It's your Mother's Day dinner. Oh, and he said to tell you 'Happy Mother's Day.'" The driver seemed a capable and enthusiastic surrogate.

It took a few seconds, then the stoic Mrs. Keegan replied "Thank you." Not clear whether it was to relay somehow magically to her son, or a mere thanks to the driver for completing the request. She rode in silence, a box of chicken in her lap, to her house on

Sycamore Street. The broad porch boasted hanging ferns and was surrounded by a freshly mulched flower bed from which spring flowers sprang and flourished. Even though Albert bought her the house, she did all her own gardening. It looked as if she lived there all her life. The driver hopped out and before he could grab the door handle, Mrs. Keegan was already popping out. "How much do I owe you?" She spoke in a straightforward, businesslike manner, opening her purse. She had a soft gentle voice. "Nothing Mam. Your son paid both ways this morning." And he added, "Oh, and he covered the chicken, too," with a smile as though he had accomplished something himself. She walked erect, handbag draped over her left arm, Hardee's box in her right hand. A glimmer of brass key stuck out of her left fingers. The cabbie watched her all the way to the door. Like an adoring movie fan watching a favorite star on Sunset Boulevard. The heavy wooden door creaked open and clunked shut. He reached in his pocket and pulled out the two twenties her son had given him. All totaled, the ride and chicken were $9.50. Just like last week.

The even light of midday gave the oak panels in the dining room a golden glow. Mrs. Keegan placed her handbag on a chair by the hallway and in four steps she set the box on the dining table. Gently, she lifted a window for fresh air and began to get the crystal, china, and linen out of the cabinet. In the kitchen she perked fresh coffee. Tenderly she cut the fried chicken with a silver knife and fork. The mashed potatoes and gravy were transferred to a crystal goblet. Never had a Hardee's chicken dinner been so elegantly served and eaten. Except for the last time Albert had sent dinner with the taxi.

And the time before that. After washing her dishes, she reclined on the couch for a nap beneath a shelf lined with old family pictures. Her wedding among them. Her deceased husband sitting at his desk. Paris. Albert's college graduation.

Afternoon birds fluttered around the feeder just outside the open window. Mrs. Keegan slept comfortably, her dress smoothed around her, her blue-gray hair crushed back on a brocade pillow. She kept her shoes on. Dreamed of vast gardens of lilies and irises, walking barefoot on long winding paths, and cool breezes sliding through her long brown hair. In the real world, coolly stalking under the boxwood by the bird feeder, Rex lay in wait. Rex, the bird killing cat that Albert had given her on her birthday last October. A small boy brought him to the front door. "Your son paid me five dollars to bring this to you." He reached out and thrust the kitty in her hands. "Oh, and he said to tell you 'Happy Birthday.'"

The screeching and tumbling outside the window startled Mrs. Keegan from her blissful slumber. She jumped off the couch like a cat herself and flung the open window higher. Rex and a cardinal flopped out from under the boxwood. A brownish female dive-bombed to protect her mate. Mrs. Keegan flung her perfectly good white pump and nailed Rex. She stood on one shoe admiring her deadeye handywork. Rex hightailed it through the shrubs and flowers and the redbird flew up to a dogwood branch to join his mate. "Fool cat," she murmured as she limped by the couch. She stopped, stepped back in her awkward one shoe tilt, reached up to Albert's picture and turned it face down on the shelf. "Fool son of mine. And oh, 'Happy Mother's Day' yourself."

perry neel

Mrs. Keegan kicked off the one shoe and barefooted outside to retrieve the other and to turn on the sprinkler. The sun was down enough now to water the lawn. Back inside, she slipped on her shoes and went to the den. Clicked on the television. It was an oversized screen for the modest den. Since the advent of cable she had trouble negotiating so many buttons and channels. But she was glad for the classic movie stations. Joan Crawford appeared on the screen and she settled into a wingchair. The volume was low, so she reached for the remote on the table. It wasn't there. Nor was it on the seat cushion beside her. She dug through a clutter of mail on the coffee table, leaned forward from the chair and stuck out one foot to gain balance. Her heel spiked the remote lying on the floor under the edge of the table. The plastic cracked. "Damn," she uttered a rare curse. Then she thought of Christmas Eve and the delivery man. "Oh, your son said to wish you a 'Merry Christmas,' Mam."

Reaching for the telephone and fumbling around her mind for Albert's number, she repeated, "8501. 5801." Since prison, he had warned her that he wanted as little contact as possible. But Mrs. Keegan could wait no longer. All the lavish gifts and attention by hire meant nothing to her. Maternal fury swelled up inside her breast. He had no right to stretch the bond of mother and child to the breaking point. It was Mother's Day after all. The least he could do....

The phone picked up after the fourth ring. She waited for the answering machine to finish. "Albert," she implored. "I know you are there. I need to talk to you." She waited. Then a click.

"OK, Mother, I'm here. What do you want?"

"Just to hear your voice, that's all. It's been two and a half years. And I have seen you, what, twice, three times? A total of five minutes."

"I know, I know."

"Can't you just come and see me for a little while?"

"But Mother...I'm simply not ready yet."

"Ready?"

"Since prison..." The meaning was understood by both. Indicated by a mutual pause.

"I know son. What do you want me to do?"

"I have to admit Mother...it's a shame. When I see you, I just can't shake the feeling..."

"I understand, son. It's alright. OK. Fine. You call me when you are ready." She really didn't want to push the issue. Maternal patience took over.

"Goodbye, Mother."

"Bye."

"And Happy Mother's Day."

"Thanks." She hung up the phone and sat on the edge of the chair. Smoothed out her dress. Got up and walked through the living room. She stopped at the shelf and gazed lovingly at the family photo display. And righted her picture of Albert. "You've been a good son, my son the attorney. Without you, I would have never gotten out of prison so soon."

perry neel

## The Man with No Ears

Joey opened the door to Buck's room, shoving back a pile of clothes and shoes that nearly blocked his entry. The sound of running water and steam seeping through the cracks around the bathroom door summoned devilish thoughts of old horror movies. A sly grin crept across Joey's face. All those pranks where he had fallen victim could now be paid back in full. He looked around the room for the tools of revenge. The trunk under the bed was where Buck kept his war machinery. Joey slid it out slowly, pried open the latches and carefully raised the lid. Hand grenades, a bazooka, an M1, GI Joe. The rubber dagger would do the trick. The addition of a Halloween mask snatched from the top book shelf, the one with stitches and gooey blood dripping from crusty gashes, should be enough to make Buck pay for all the words he heaped on Joey about being a coward and a sissy. The tables turned. Long overdue payback was coming.

Easing through the bathroom door, barely seeing out the little slits of the rubber mask, Joey raised the dagger high. Excitement pounded in his chest. His face sweated from the steam penetrating the rubber mask. He could see Joey's silhouette through the brightly colored dinosaur shower curtain. Before the attack, he quickly scrawled a message of doom with his finger on the mirror. "Buck must die!" Gently, Joey tiptoed through the puddles on the grid tile floor. Suddenly, "I'm Popeye the sailor man. I live in a garbage can..." Buck's singing caught him by surprise and he nearly slipped trying to duck down low. Luckily, Buck was caught up in his own performance. He gripped a bar of soap like a microphone. All the better for distraction.

Joey crawled around the old claw-foot tub to get to the back side, on his hands and knees, rubber dagger clinched between his teeth. There he caught a full view of his victim through the clear part of the curtain.

"I'm Popeye the sailor man, I live in a frying pan..." "Now I've got you," Joey relished the moment, slowly pulling back the curtain, ready to plunge the knife with Norman Bates' fervor into his unwitting victim. "I turn all the switches and burn up my britches..." Buck continued to croon. Now up on one knee, Joey stuck his face through the curtain, poised to spring the attack. But his advance was suddenly thwarted. He crumpled to the floor, belly heaving with a howling laugh. Joey's cheeks reddened, his teeth shining. The rubber knife rolled on the wet floor. There stood Buck, in the shower, wearing a raincoat, hat, and boots.

"Ha, ha, haha!" Joey hadn't yet found the disappointment of his lost revenge. The sight of Buck in yellow rubber raingear instantly struck his funny bone. He rolled on the floor like a lunatic. "You idiot!" Buck jumped and screamed in terror. "I oughta kill you, you little bastard." He reached down, water running off his raincoat, and snatched the monster mask off Joey's head like plucking a dandelion. Buck tried never to show fear. Big, tough guys don't. He would never let on that Joey had scared the wits out of him. Joey lay in the puddle, giggling, tears now rolling down his cheeks. "You've had a good laugh. Now get up! And gimme that knife." Buck hurled it at the door as though it would stick in it, Indian style. It bounced like a stiff fish over behind the toilet. Joey giggled, still floundering on the floor. Buck held him with one hand, collared by his t-shirt.

Joey admired Buck. Buck was his hero, even though he was always treated like a kid. They were the same age. It wasn't really fair. Buck liked to tease him. A hundred million pranks played on him. Still, Joey liked him. Buck was a natural born leader. And Joey, a natural born follower. That sometimes meant being the butt of a joke. Or having your revenge backfire. Even though he harbored the thought that maybe he really did terrify Buck just this one time. But he knew his buddy would never own up to it. It wasn't his nature. Still, Buck was his protector. It meant being free from the hassle of bullies. And a chance to admire girls from up close. They flocked to Buck. Joey was always embarrassed. He would never even touch a girl. But he like being close enough to smell one. They always smelled nice and sweet to him. And money. Buck seemed to have an infinite supply. Unlike most twelve year olds. Always sharing sodas and candy bars at the drug store after school. So Joey looked forward to high school, certain that Buck would be the first kid to get a car, and that he, Joey, would be riding around in it blowing dust on the other guys and offering rides to pretty girls.

"Buck, why are you wearing a raincoat in the shower?" Joey managed between depleting chuckles.

"Never mind that," Buck redirected. "Did you get a picture of him yet?"

perry neel

"No, I couldn't sneak Mom's camera out of her room."

"Why not?"

"She said she had a headache and laid down on the bed."

"Well, you seem pretty good at creeping around without other people knowing it." Buck sloshed water off his hat at Joey.

Joey picked up the rubber mask and turned it inside out, slipping it over his head while Buck took off his raincoat only to find his clothes wet. "Why were you in the shower with your clothes on," Joey tried again.

"It's a deal with my mother. She says I have to take a shower every day or I'll go around stinking."

"Like Plank," Joey inquired.

"Yeah, like Plank. But this is an experiment I've got going. If I shower in my raincoat for a week, and my mother doesn't know it, and if she never says I stink, then I can tell her I really wasn't taking a shower all week when she thought I was. So, I don't need to take one every day. See?"

"If you say so, Buck." Joey stuck his tongue out through the mouth slit of the monster mask.

Buck dried off with a Bart Simpson beach towel while Joey rummaged through comic books on the bed. Buck looked up from buffing his ears. "We gotta get that picture of Plank."

Joey rolled over on his back. "But he won't let anybody close to him. Besides, I'm scared of him. And I like having ears." Joey's voice crackled a little.

"That's just what those old day laborers down on Dock Street told you," Buck countered. "They don't know what happened to

118

Plank's ears. They're just trying to pull one over on you. They know you are scared."

"But I heard he listened in on some men in Henley's garage planning a bank robbery. They found out because he stepped on a broken bottle out in the alley and it cut through his thin old shoe. When he hollered, they ran outside the garage and grabbed Plank. Took him down to the lake and chopped off his ears with a hatchet."

"Nonsense. You can't believe those old guys. They sit around making up tales all day. Listen, Jimmy says his cousin writes for this big magazine in Atlanta. They will pay us good money for a story about the man with no ears. But we have to have a picture to prove there is such a man. Plank goes around all day with that scarf around his head, under that old hat pulled down real low. Even when it's hot. If we can just figure out how to get his picture without all that stuff on his head, then maybe we can find out what happened to his ears. Listen, little shit, I'll have me that car when I'm 16. The means we'll have us a car. Hell, we can drive it this year. There'll be enough money to pay off the cops if they pull us over."

"How we gonna drive it? Neither one of us know how." Joey leaned on his elbows, crumpling down comic books in the sagging mattress.

"We'll hire us a driver, then. Until we are old enough." Buck tugged on a pair of jeans and wiggled down a gray sweatshirt over his chest. "Then you and me, kiddo, we'll be kings of the road. The girls will love us." That is the part Joey liked to hear. He couldn't even speak to a girl. In fact, it had been since second grade the last time he had spoken to one. "I think we need to catch old Plank," Buck continued, "when he comes out of Grayson's Alley with that bag of booze under his arm. You come up to him like you are beggin' for money or something. Have the camera under your jacket. Then I'll jump out from behind the fence around the garbage cans at Fellini's Deli and snatch the hat and scarf off his head. You take the picture. We'll just make up some story to tell the people from the magazine. And we'll pick out a car that afternoon!"

"Don't you think we oughta really find out what happened to Plank's ears?"

"Heck no. What do you think they'll do, go ask him? He won't talk to nobody anyway. They'll never know. We'll just make up something that sounds good."

"But don't you want to know? I do. Maybe he was hunting lions in Africa or in one of those wars we read about in school."

"You know," Buck started with that mature looking gleam in his eyes, the kind that Joey couldn't quite understand. He always assumed Buck was more familiar with the world of adults. "I heard there was some girl down at Lang's Bar, they said she could screw the ears right off a man. Maybe that's what happened?" Joey didn't want to admit that he wasn't sure what "screw" meant.

Shaking his head as he spoke, Joey queried, "Wouldn't that hurt?" He envisioned twisting Plank's ears off, as if they were threaded on. He wondered if that was what Buck did to him whenever he grabbed and twisted his ears on those red cold winter mornings. Mornings when he ignored his mother's advice to wear a hat.

"Tomorrow," Buck intoned with dead serious eyes, the kind he would use when teachers suspected him of trouble and he'd make up some outlandish, yet believable excuse. "Meet me at 6:30 in the morning in front of Fellini's. We'll stake out the alley just like I said." With a snatch of Joey's collar, he drew him close, eyeball to eyeball. "And don't forget the camera. Or I'll tell Miss Green about you peeking through her window while she was changing clothes."

"But that was you," Joey garbled as Buck tightened the grip on his shirt. Joey understood. He hadn't the nerve to climb up the rose trellis at Miss Green's, their art teacher's house. Buck climbed it like a monkey. But Buck could somehow twist a story around. He'd make Joey the guilty party. And even he would end up believing it. "I'll be there," he hesitated, "with the camera."

*    *    *    *    *    *    *    *    *

Joey leaned against the brownstone front of Fellini's Deli. He reached up with a mittened hand to wipe the sleep from his eyes. Then he blew his foggy breath onto the mitten to watch the water droplets condense on the wooly hairs. Under his down jacket he clutched the instamatic camera he had smuggled from his mother's room while she was still sleeping. A small bruise marked his forehead where he caught the edge of the nightstand while crawling in the dark. A few cars rolled quietly down the street in the gray early morning. No one in a hurry to get to work. Puddles of water reflected the grayness of the sky. A silent dark figure moved quietly down the sidewalk across the street. At times he would pause at one of the skinny maples planted along the side of the road. Joey, ever the young scientist, continued to focus on the microcosm of the world formed in the condensation on his mitten. The figure darted across the street just behind a rumbling station wagon and lurked underneath the storefront awnings. Joey was amazed at the tiny droplets dangling on the ends of each wool hair, wondering if they would freeze into little iceballs if it were colder.

Suddenly a hand grabbed Joey's experimental mitten and a voice shrilled "You look hungry little boy, have a doughnut," and a great wad of yeasty bread and sugary glaze with an ooze of red jelly slammed into his face. Stunned and sticky, Joey reeled back against the plate glass window, hard enough to bounce back a little. Buck stood bent over, moaning heavily with laughter, his unbuttoned, olive drab, army issue overcoat flapping with each shrug. Joey, being a great fan of jelly doughnuts, was not one to let his shock from the sneak attack prevent him from enjoying the delicious raspberry filling. His blue mitten swept across his face, shoving the smear of doughnut into his mouth.

"Did you bring the camera, moron?" Buck instantly turned serious. The demeanor of a commando setting out on a mission. A mercenary awaiting the great reward to follow a successful expedition. Joey pushed the lump under his jacket indicating the hidden camera. "Good. If he's still sleeping in the old body shop at the other end of Grayson's Alley, then maybe he'll get up and check out Fellini's trash for some leftover meatballs or something for breakfast with his booze. I'll hide behind the garbage cans. You hit him up for spare change."

"But I have..." Joey caught himself being too literal. "Do you think he'll believe I really need money? He doesn't look like the kind you go begging to, either. Seems pretty poor to me." Before he could go on, he caught that look from Buck that said without saying, "Are you stupid or what?"

"Does it really matter," Buck growled. "It doesn't take a scientist to figure this out. You just gotta get his attention. I'll jump out and grab his hat, pull off his scarf, and you snap the picture." As an afterthought, he added, "And we run like hell."

Joey's stomach sank with the sudden fear that camera may not have any film. He forgot to check. Quickly he felt through the hole in his jacket pocket and turned the advance knob. No film! How could he tell Buck? The plan was already in motion. And it had zero chance for success. None, and he knew it. His lips were frozen. Then Buck took him by the arm and led him toward the alley. Joey remained calm on the outside, but inwardly he wanted to fly off in retreat, a coward on the battlefield. Advance to the rear. His mind reeled through the million tortures and the thousand deaths Buck would rain down on him. But the plot was unfolding too quickly now. Before he knew it, Buck had positioned him, whispering final instructions. Then in the distance, a solitary man, brown bag under one arm, lifting trash can lids with the other, trudged down the alleyway. He displayed a kind of politeness, gently lifting and returning each lid quietly. A weathered brown hat perched on his head. A dark plaid scarf hung down both sides of his head, running down under the collar of his shabby woolen coat. It was Plank.

Buck stood poised behind the fence that obscured the trash from the street. Joey's stomach quivered. As soon as Plank reached the cans, Joey robotically walked up with his hand out. So original for a twelve year old, "Buddy can you spare a dime?" He didn't realize he had ever heard those words before. In a whirlwind of action, Buck dive-bombed from the top of the fence, screeching like an attacking hawk. Plank growled and swung around his free arm. He missed and staggered from his flail. He swung wildly again. Joey crumpled to the sidewalk from the blow. The brown hat lay flattened beside him. With the action moving so fast, Joey still managed to pull out the camera and flashed it right up in Plank's face. He'd forgotten how futile all of this was already rendered. By the time he remembered there was no film, he re-established his goal to fool Buck. The camera's flash at least could buy him some time. The sudden blur of action now stilled. Plank scurried up the alley reinstalling his scarf and hat, careful to hold onto the paper sack. Buck lay sideways on the ground.

"Are you OK?" Joey pleaded as he knelt down to attend to Buck. Maybe Plank had knifed him, or shot him, or kung fued him to death. "Did you get him?" Buck shot up from his position on the ground as if only momentarily stunned by a Martian ray gun. "Yeah, I think so," Joey displayed his uncertainty. "You think so?!" Buck demanded more than questioned. Joey quickly lied. "Yeah, I got him good. No ears and all." He knew he would have to figure his way out of this later.

\*     \*     \*     \*     \*     \*     \*     \*     \*

"Clank-clink-clink" the Coke can tumbled, pummeled to a dented mass by Joey's repeated kicks. He stood by the rail of the 14th Street bridge as the can slowly teetered over the edge with a little nudge from his toe. All he could think about was the four dollars Buck had given him to take to the drug store for the one day film processing. He felt the bills jumbled up in his pocket. Buck had been jubilant that at last they had the picture. And the story they would concoct about the man with no ears would bring them wealth and fame. Joey felt sick. He was glad Buck did not stick around and eventually force a confession. He said something about going down to the car lot and look for a beauty! Joey was not sure if he meant a blond or a Firebird. It no longer mattered. "What am I going to tell Buck. He'll kill me. He'll worse than kill me."

Crossing the bridge he turned up Atmore Street along a row of abandoned store fronts. He pulled down the edge of his mitten to check his Superman wristwatch. 10:36. The sign at the photo shop said "In by 9, back by 4." Buck would be there waiting. Promptly at 4. Waiting for nothing. Joey knew that he would not be there. He reached into his jacket pocket to pull out the four dollars. All wadded in a ball. It hit him like a flash. Joey took off up Atwood and back down Mason Lane. The bus station.

He hurried up to the ticket window and plunked down the ball of four dollar bills. He pulled them apart to show the man. "Where will this take me?" "It will get you to Blairsburg, son. But why would you want to go there?" the ticket agent smiled suspiciously at the little boy. Joey wondered if he had an electric button under to counter to silently call the police and let them know a kid was about to run away. He snatched the money and ran for the terminal exit, between a couple of idling buses and down a back alley. Out of breath and wheezing, he stopped at a pile of rubble behind an old building. Took a seat on a concrete block and panted like an old dog. "What will I do?" he shook his head.

He sat while time rolled and no ideas came to him. He knew he had to get away from town, from Buck, by 4 p.m. Joey gasped suddenly as he felt a hand on his shoulder. He wheeled around so quickly that he fell off the block and out of the clutching hand. Plank stood over him. Paper bag in one hand, hat and scarf over his head. He grunted a few sounds Joey couldn't make out. Joey tried to let out a muffled scream but his fear had swollen like a walnut in his throat. Plank thrust out a hand. The flash of something shiny made him think a gun or a knife. It was a quarter. Plank again uttered unintelligibly. Sounded like he might be saying, "Take it." The face of the man offering the coin looked almost kind. Joey slowly rose to his feet. Not knowing what to do, he reached out to take the coin. Plank then pulled up a concrete block and sat down. His face was brown and smooth. His eyes sad, a dull brown. Everything about him was brown. His clothes, his hat, his shoes, dusty brown. Only the dark plaid scarf showed some lines of blue and green. He reached in his sack and pulled out some bread. Probably part of a loaf thrown out at Fellini's. He sat silently and ate without offering Joey a piece. As if he knew no one would want bread fished from a garbage can. Joey sat down on his block. He looked at Plank's sack. It contained, for all he knew, all of Plank's worldly possessions. A comb. A small transistor radio. Some scraps of paper. A bottle of cheap wine with only a couple of swallows left in it. A plastic flower.

Joey wanted to speak but didn't know what to say. Maybe Plank really thought he was begging when Buck jumped him. Maybe that is why he offered the quarter. Did he not see the camera and figure it was a setup?

Finally words came to him. An obvious question, but words. "You are Plank, aren't you?" The man stared blankly. With the characteristic innocence, yet boldness of a child, Joey continued. "They say you are the man with no ears. Now I don't know if that's true. I've never seen your ears," pausing before adding, "or the lack of them." Plank looked at him as if he understood. But Joey wondered if he could hear. "Some of the guys say awful things about how you lost your ears. That is, if you really lost them. I hope no one has hurt your feelings if you really don't have any...ears that is. I know you got feelings." He turned the quarter over in his hand. Only a man with feelings would offer a boy money.

"Do you mind if I see them? I'm just curious, that's all. I won't take your picture or anything." He was embarrassed now that he had revealed the plot. He held out empty hands as if to show he had no weapons. Without hesitating, Plank reached up with leathery hands and politely took off his hat. He put it upside down on the ground. Then with the humbleness of a patient showing his injury to a doctor, he lowered his scarf. He had ears. At least parts of ears. They looked mangled. More melted. Quickly, without a sound he wrapped his head again and topped it with the brown hat. He reached into his sack, pulled out a piece of paper, and handed it to Joey. A big coin or something fell out on the ground. It shined of gold for a second, but Plank snatched it up and shoved it back in the sack. The piece of paper was old. A newspaper clipping, yellow and worn. The headline read "Man Risks Life to Save Children from Fire." The caption under a picture of a man lying on a stretcher, his head and hands bandaged, said "Local Hero Seriously Injured While Making Daring Rescue." Then another clipping, apparently later. The photo showed a man receiving a medallion from the mayor of the city. It was too dark to even make out the man's face. Plank looked down at the ground the whole time Joey read. He dusted crumbs from his brown clothes and reached for the clippings. It seemed like he had a time limit on how long he would share them. Plank thrust them deep into the brown paper bag, stood up and turned to walk back down the alley. His head lowered, his left foot dragging slightly. He walked quietly, peacefully, sometimes stopping to take a poke in a garbage can.

Joey crossed the 14th Street bridge and stopped to look across the river. A couple of joggers passed by, wearing shorts and tank tops even in the winter chill. Trash floated, bobbing down the river. A man sat on an old tire on the bank across the way. Attempting to fish, or at least kill time in solitude. The sun was shining brightly like a gold medal in the sky. He wondered if Plank could hear out of those crumpled ears. He wondered if he could speak more than a few grunts. He wondered what it meant to be a hero.

CPSIA information can be obtained at www.ICGtesting.com
Printed in the USA
BVOW03s0927191214

379956BV00005B/10/P

9 781499 556490